Ties tha

CW01483722

by

John Gent

A RedPen Publication 2008

Dedications
and
Acknowledgements

This book could not have been written without the help and guidance of so many people. Family, friends, and especially the Spiritualist movement.

A serious health problem forced me on a journey. A quest. I sought relief, comfort, and answers, at the most crucial time in my life.

Demons of the mind threatened my daily existence.

The problems I faced aren't rare. The disease is spreading, Universally. Mankind is terminally ill. Greed, anger and selfishness are killing us all. Anxiety and stress levels are at an all time high, unseen enemies of the human race; potentially as destructive as any physical ailments.

I hope, and pray, that this novel will help you, the reader, to find your own answers, solutions to the Cancer of the Soul.

Opening the mind to the possibility of an existence beyond the grave *will* change your life, for the better; as it did mine.

The story about the Brooks family is fiction. But my ten years involvement in the Spiritualist Religion has produced many of the scenarios depicted.

Have an open mind and an open heart. As Mrs. Harwood says:

'Let the message be the proof.'

P.S. Thank you Spirit.

J. Gent

ISBN 978-0-9560870-0-3

Ties that Bind

Chapter 1

"God give me strength. Why me?" Miriam asked the ten by eight photograph gripped in trembling hands.

"Accident, how *dare* they say it was an accident. He *killed* my son, they should've locked him up and thrown the key away."

The Coroner judged that the Transit van had collided with Jeremy's car, but conflicting evidence regarding the traffic light indication had to be taken into account; the only safe conclusion was a verdict of accidental death. A recommendation to the Highways Authority advising immediate upgrading of the junction was duly recorded.

"An eye for an eye and a tooth for a tooth, that's what the Lord said."

"Where's me dinner?" Fred shouted from the kitchen, at least it rescued Miriam from the dark depths of despair and self pity. Fred never realised he shouted, how loud his voice could get. An accident at work did the damage, almost deaf in the right ear ever since.

He was in the middle of a frustrating search, his chip pan was missing; possibly hidden. Miriam didn't believe in frying the chips anymore, decreeing that if he would insist on having the fried version with all the nasty cholesterol, he'd have to cook them; or resort to the much healthier oven variety.

"There it is," the deep fat fryer was found, concealed behind a mountain of pans. "Miriam!" He tutted, placing the source of many an argument on the stove. "I blame them bloody TV cooks. No fat, no lard. Ya can't cook chips wi'out lard; better still beef drippin.' Bland and tasteless. Yuk. Give me good old fashioned snap anytime. Miriam, do ya want owt?"

Not on your life, she decided. Not wanting to upset him she simply answered, "No, not just yet thank you."

She'd nicknamed her partner of forty two years Victor, after the grumpy Meldrew character on TV. That said, Miriam wouldn't have been at all amused with the nom de plume Fred had chosen for her. Under his breath, when mentioning Miriam's many failings to his beloved pigeons, she was Nigella.

He could watch the sultry TV cook all day, in between the horse racing coverage of course, mixing the exotic ingredients, hungrily tasting morsels of food from those long, sensual, sensitive fingers. He wouldn't have eaten any of it, but Ding Dong, Nigella could feel free to use his chip pan anytime she wanted.

Chip pans and cooking apart nothing was the same since their son Jeremy died. Fred mused, checking the temperature of the demon fat. What a tragic waste of life. Thirty five and never married, Jeremy favouring the single status, fancy cars, fancy women, holidays to match, of course. What a terrible waste. If only, if only, if only.

They still had Julia, the youngest. She was a mistake; Miriam's polite way of saying they hadn't used a contraceptive.

Did it matter? After all Julia was a little angel, always had been. A perfect pregnancy culminated in a small baby at six pounds eight ounces. The complication free delivery was bang on the date predicted, and wonder of wonders, she slept all through the night.

Jeremy had been a problem from birth. Seven days overdue, he came into the world weighing almost ten pounds, a difficult birth. Yes, an understatement. Damage was done in the process.

"I'm having no more. You can have the next one." Miriam squealed at Fred as she was prepared for the repair job.

"You may need sixteen stitches Mrs. Brooks. I'm sorry, it may hurt." The little Asian nurse involuntarily winced at the thought.

Fred said they should have put twenty stitches in. Fred did like a joke.

****

"Take me to our Julia's." Miriam urged Fred, "I must talk to someone."

Fred had long since accepted he didn't qualify as someone. Since the accident an emotional gap had widened between them. The subject couldn't be mentioned without tears and shouting. He missed their son just as much, but had difficulty showing his feelings. Sooner than argue, he jumped into the Ford Focus and taxied Miriam to Selston, where Julia lived.

His main function would be to drop Miriam off and wait for a phone call. What's more Templegate, the racing guru in the daily paper said there was a dead cert in the 3'oclock at Sandown, and Fred would kick himself if he missed it. Anyway, they didn't need a bloke who didn't talk their language.

****

"We should go to Hasland church, *bound* to help us in our loss. That's what Mrs. Roberts says." Julia massaged her mother's arthritic tortured hands with moisturising lotion.

"I didn't know there was a church in Hasland. Ooh Julia, I like this new cream you got me. Smells like coconut, leaves my hands all soft and warm."

Julia smiled, her open face a joy to see. In order to cover herself for any later disappointments should they ever decide to visit the church, she quickly added, "Well. It's more like a shed really. Yeah, apparently a lot of Spiritualist Churches are small flimsy structures. They even hold services in Youth Centres and community rooms."

Miriam sat upright on the settee, withdrawing her hands from her daughter's grip. "I'm *not* going in a shed; I learnt that lesson the hard way. I was only fourteen at the time. Billy Murphy said he wanted to show me something in his dad's garden shed. Ugh, I won't forget that in a hurry. No thank you."

"Mum it's all right; I went there just after Jeremy died."

Miriam's eyebrows shot up. "*Where*? Old man Murphy's shed! *Y'never* did our Julia."

"No Mam, don't be silly. I meant to *Hasland*."

"Well thank the Lord for that, you had me worried there, but you never told me about your church visit."

"I didn't think you were ready. It was early days, only a short while after the funeral. You cried spontaneously at everything."

"Of course I did. I missed him."

"We all missed him Mum. Even Dad."

"You'll understand if you ever have children; it's like part of you as died."

She'd said the dreaded word, died. Each time she said it made it more final. She still couldn't accept it.

"Stop crying Mum. You'll make yourself ill."

"Pass me a tissue please." Miriam sobbed.

Julia hated to see her mum cry. "Do you need a tablet? A drink of water?"

"Just pass me my handbag Pet. The pills are in the side pocket."

The last time she'd called Julia 'Pet' was at the inquest; after the coroner formally announced, "Case closed; no further action to be taken."

Resignation, not acceptance. The pain would never go away; there would always be the emptiness.

"Is that any better? Do you want to lie down?" Julia moved the cushions on the settee.

"Just give me a minute love, they'll kick in shortly."

She hated taking the pills. She knew Lorazapams were addictive, but she needed them. They eased her shaking body, calmed the broken heart trying to jump out of her chest.

Miriam composed herself by stroking the silver coloured ring hanging on a chain round her neck. "What happens at these Spiritualist places?"

"I only went the once and I was bored." Julia appeared as if she'd been let down by the experience, that it hadn't lived up to her expectations. "They said a prayer or two, sang a few hymns. Apart from the bit when this old woman stood up there talking to herself, it was like going to the Methodist chapel in King Street."

"*Talked* to herself?" Miriam looked puzzled.

"Well. She was alone on the platform, but kept saying, '*All right, take your time, I can only do one at once.*'"

"And there was no one there?"

Julia responded by pulling a face, almost as if she implied something wasn't quite right at the meeting.

"Was she mad? Did they drag her away in a straightjacket?"

"The funny thing was, everybody I spoke to said she was brilliant."

"Go on."

"Yes. Mrs. Roberts from the butchers in the High Street was told by the medium - apparently these crazy people who talk to invisible dead people are called mediums - that her Ted was with her."

"But Ted's been dead for years."

"Exactly."

"So what did you do?"

"I had a cup of tea and a biscuit, I think it's a tradition in these sheds."

"No wonder you didn't tell me, it wouldn't have helped at all."

5

"Yes. But Mother, I'm saving the best to the last. Mrs. Roberts also said Mrs. Harwood, the crazy medium, was awesome."

"Awesome? How do you mean awesome?"

"That's what Mrs. Roberts told me. The medium told her all sorts of things, like Ted having a wooden leg, caused by shrapnel in the war. Said he'd passed in the October month."

Miriam was starting to get interested. Not in the wooden leg, though in itself it sounded fascinating, but the passing bit. "She actually said *passing* our Julia?"

"Yes passing. Apparently there is no death. We all pass on to the Summerland."

Chapter 2

"Harold, you're spoiling that child. You'll regret it one day. Mark my words." This was a typical Audrey Haslam response to anything nice that Harold did for their daughter.

"Bloody hell Audrey, give it a rest will you. And don't talk so loud, she'll hear you." Harold looked through the window.

Miriam was playing with the kitten. Cute little thing. Jumping in and out of her arms, racing through the bed of flowers, climbing up the stalks until they collapsed under the weight of the feline lumberjack.

"She needs a companion. She's got no friends, I blame you for that Audrey."

"Of course you do, you blame me for everything."

"Don't say another word." Harold stared directly into his wife's clear blue eyes, deep, cold, and menacing. Breaking away from the visual battle he placed his pipe on the mantel-piece. He took a slow deep breath, quenching the anger about to explode from his lips.

"I *know* you blame me, you just don't say it." Audrey had finally thrown down the gauntlet.

It had taken five years of festering anger and despair to reach this point. The confrontation.

"He was *my* son as much as yours." Harold turned, resuming the face-off, clenched fists secured by his side.

"I carried the twins for eight months, I held him as the life slipped away from his tiny body." Tears flooded down Audrey's face, now a grotesque mask of muscular spasms. "*You* were too busy with *her*."

"Don't exaggerate and distort the truth, you know it wasn't like that. He had severe complications, he wouldn't have survived long no matter what the surgeons did. They explained it all to us. At least Miriam had a chance to live. The incubator saved her life." Harold was crying. Slumping into a chair he rested his head on his hands, tears dripping between his fingers onto the tablecloth.

Audrey composed herself. Taking a lace hankie from the linen drawer she methodically dabbed away any evidence of emotional failure from her pale face.

"He was too beautiful to live, the midwife said so." Tucking the hankie into her left sleeve she approached her husband.

"Isaac David died and Miriam Mary lived. End of. I can't help how I feel about her."

Harold sat up, ignoring his tears he looked up at Audrey, "You could *try,* you don't have to make it so obvious, she knows you don't love her."

"She'll get over it. You can love her enough for both of us." Audrey moved to the sink. Dinner to get ready.

****

Harold never did regret anything he did for Miriam.

She had a difficult childhood, missing the guidance of a loving mother, but Audrey was right; he did love her enough for both of them. They got through.

Miriam, no academic genius failed the eleven plus; depending on the viewpoint either a good or bad outcome.

****

Audrey never took to Freddy Brooks, blaming South Normanton Secondary Modern for bringing the young lad into the picture. Harold didn't agree with Audrey's opinion, as usual. He saw a hidden side to his daughter's choice of companion. Behind Fred's rough and ready exterior beat a good heart, he sensed it.

8

Harold trusted his intuitions, what he called his gut feelings. They'd proven worthy and pertinent on many occasions.

"She's far too good for the likes of him," Audrey said. "His dad's a miner, filthy job." She shuddered at the very thought of it.

"If men like Fred's dad didn't risk their lives everyday going to the depths of the earth we'd all be in a sorry state. You'd be the first to complain Audrey. No open fire to keep you warm, no electricity for lighting and telly. Imagine that before you condemn the lad. Or his dad"

"Do they have to get so dirty?"

"Getting dirty is the least of their worries. Somebody brought the Coal News into the office last week. The report was in about the explosion at Sutton Colliery."

"I saw it in the Mail, Brierley Colliery they called it."

"Aye, the locals do call it that. Did you know that five men died? Another twenty were seriously injured by the flames and gases; just so we can have proper toast and you can watch Emergency - Ward 10."

"You like your toast and telly as much as I do, I have to drag you from that sofa to the table when Danger Man's on, it's like you're glued to the seat."

"*Awright*, leave off. What I'm trying to tell you is that Freddy's dad does a very dangerous job so that the likes of us can enjoy the comforts of his labours. If he ever comes here I'll shake his hand. Mucky or not." Harold sounded annoyed: she knew she may have overstepped the mark.

"Oh don't make such a big thing about it, she'll more than likely finish with him next week."

"That just shows how much you know our daughter. When she started to wash her hair every Friday night I knew it was serious."

"That's my Bingo night, how would I know?"

"You'd know if you wanted to know. You'd make it your

business. I bet you don't know she wears lipstick when she goes out."

Audrey stopped her sewing, flashed a thunderous look straight at Harold. "The *little* hussy, where does she get that from?"

"Certainly not from you. Her mate Rita carries some in her handbag. They put it on when they get to the Youth Club."

"You seem to be well informed. Why don't you tell her off? She'll listen to you. Stop her going out with that Rita Jones. Her mum was a right slapper."

"It's innocent enough, she's a good girl. I trust her."

"Well I don't. The first time I see a love bite on her neck she's in for it."

"It wasn't her fault her brother died. We've had that one out before.

"Don't start that again. Play a different tune will you. Leave it." Audrey hated the subject.

"I will if you will. Let her get on with it. I like Freddy." Harold rustled his newspaper hinting there should be an end to it.

And there was.

****

So Miriam did marry Fred, who decided that Freddy wasn't appropriate anymore, too childish, him being a grown man and working at coal face and all.

Miriam looked radiant in white, sparkling blue eyes glowing with happiness.

The reception was held at the Miners Welfare. Audrey wasn't happy at the choice of venue. Her suggestion that they used Shirland Country Golf Club for the celebrations being unanimously overruled by the other interested parties. Mr. and

Mrs. Brooks said that as they were paying half of the expenses they should have a say in the way it was spent. A compromise was reached. The wedding could be held at St. Helens Church instead of Mansfield Registry Office, but the limited funds remaining would be best spent at the Welfare.

Five of the six major voters were very content. Tough on Audrey. With such a tight budget it had to be used wisely.

"Do I have to sit between them?" Audrey ventured, screwing her nose in disgust.

"No, you can sit in the toilet if you want." By then Harold was losing his patience. He never realised what a snob his wife had become. "They'll be wearing proper suits you know. The same as mine. They'll be leaving the pit muck and working clothes at home."

Audrey shut up; aware she'd fought a losing battle.

****

Young Fred had joined his dad at the pit, A Winning Colliery, on leaving school. A secure job with good prospects. After a long engagement the subject of marriage and starting a family was discussed. Miriam agreed on one condition, they must have somewhere to live. "Our own place," she'd insisted.

She'd have been happy to stay with Fred's parents until they could afford their own place, but the end terrace was too small to accommodate two families. Living with her own parents in the large three bed detached on Albert Street, was not on option; in fact it would have been over her dead body, and Fred's.

On the day the NCB Housing Association allocated number 9 Pit Row to the young couple the wedding day was set. The future Mr. and Mrs. Brooks, junior, were well chuffed.

Of course the reception was a great success; helped considerably by the magnificent fruit punch mixture. The concoction started out as three parts lemonade, one part pineapple juice and one part white wine, with apple and orange slices placed around the rim for effect. The problems started when the lemonade ran out.

Sooner than disappoint the ladies, the men quite happy with the Mansfield Bitter, some wise albeit inebriated moron decided to add another clear liquid that looked just like lemonade. Coming from a bottle emblazoned with Smirnoff in large red letters, it became an instant success.

Audrey was partial to a tipple, and known to have a dry white wine on her way home from the Bingo, she blamed her friends of course; a bad influence that lot. Naturally she went back for several refills. She danced with Fred senior, Harold danced with Ethel. The magic punch formula certainly reached the parts flattery never could.

"We must get together again. Next week sometime." Audrey apparently said, doing the injured penguin walk to the taxi waiting to convey the senior Mr. and Mrs. Brooks home. Audrey always denied the suggestion afterwards. The reunion never materialised anyway.

The newlyweds spent their first night in the White Lion Inn, any lack of luxurious linen and accessories in the boudoir never noticed. They only had eyes for each other, as one might read within the pages of a romantic novel.

The cold light of morning revealed a surprise. Miriam had woken several times in the night with a gentle breathing sound in her ear, thinking it was Fred's insatiable appetite for her charms, she pulled away, saying. "I think you've had enough Fred. Save a bit for tomorrow."

She rose at six thirty in the morning to answer a call of nature.

Swinging out of the bed-sheets she was startled by a noise; the landlord's guinea pig falling onto the floor. All romantic interpretations of being Fred's sweet nothings instantly shattered.

Guinea pig or not within a year she was with child. Happily so. She swore to Fred that whatever she had it would be loved. At seven months into the pregnancy she gave up her secretarial job in Pinxton Clothing Apparel and became a full time housewife. She never did full time work again. Her family was more important.

Chapter 3

"Bloody Templegate." Fred moaned to his fellow victim Harry. They ripped up the betting slips and threw them into the nearest waste bin, already half full. He'd donated another twenty quid to the Ladbrokes benevolent fund. Harry had obliged with his fiver. Tight Git.

The sure thing and nap of the day beaten into third place.

"Even Lester Piggott couldn't have won on *that* donkey. Came out of the stalls on its knees. He only wanted a shovel and he could've worked on the coal face with us."

"Now then Victor," Harry cautiously said to his mate of twenty years at the pit. "Don't be such a bad loser. We'll get it back tomorrow; we've only *lent* it to em."

"That's why they need these bloody jumbo size bins." Fred snarled. "And *don't* call me Victor. I'm nothing like him. *I don't believe it.*"

The overture to *Carmen* exploded from Fred's mobile phone, ending the discussion. It was time to pick Nigella up. The latest electronic toy was a reluctant purchase, not his scene at all, too *high tec*. But it served as a lifeline, an instant contact with Miriam when she needed him. No one else knew the number, or that he used it to take pictures of Frankie, his favourite racing pigeon.

He'd chosen this tune because it reminded him of better times. Barely three years ago, it seemed like an eternity, he'd taken Miriam to London to see the Bizet classic at the Royal Opera House. That Maria Ewing sure was fit. Yeah, happier times.

"I'll be there in ten minutes. Put the kettle on," he whispered into the mouthpiece, not wanting half of Pinxton knowing his business.

****

"Ya doing me head in our Julia. Don't ya encourage ya mam."

Talk of the dead and contacting them, was over Fred's head. It gave him the jitters.

Miriam stared hard at him, but for Julia's sake kept silent; let her daughter tell this obstinate man what it was all about, the good Lord knows she couldn't without losing her temper. First it was the chip pan argument and now this lot.

"Just drink your Yorkshire tea and shut up Dad," Julia snapped." Think of Mum for once."

Now that hurt. They knew he'd severe limitations in accepting the Unknown. He was a Sagittarian after all.

"You pair have watched that bloody film *Sixth Sense* too many times."

"*Dad*. That was fiction. This is fact."

"*Fac*t. Lass, I'm almost drawing me pension and ya ask me ta believe this rubbish. How can it be fact when only mad people and witches say they can talk to the dead."

He was growing agitated. His large fingers drummed on the kitchen table.

"They used to burn them at the stake, ya know." He would have said more but priority went to the Hob-Nob biscuit slipping from his grip, almost drowning in the amber waters.

"If your reading material was expanded beyond the *Pigeon Racing Weekly* and *The Sun*, you might know better. The Witchcraft Act was actually repealed in the fifties," Julia said, spitefully removing the biscuit barrel out of her stubborn father's reach.

Miriam decided to interrupt. "I'm going to see Mrs. Harwood. I've been told she does private sittings at her home. *I know* she can help me."

"I bet she can for twenty quid a session." Fred scoffed after being told the fee.

"She lives in Derby, near Markeaton Park." Julia was doing all she could to bring some comfort and relief to her mum. She hoped Mrs. Harwood was the answer.

"I dare bet she escaped from Mickleover." Fred sniggered.

Geographically the village of Mickleover was only two miles down the road from the picturesque Markeaton Park. Locally it still carried the stigma of once housing a lunatic asylum.

"The mental institution was officially called the Pastures. The council converted it into flats years ago," Julia primly informed the scowling Fred.

"*So*. That don't mean she wasn't a patient there."

"Stop it Dad. You're not at all funny. Grow up."

"I'm not bothered what he thinks." Miriam said raising her voice. "*Julia*, make me an appointment as soon as possible. I need all the help I can get."

She cast a demeaning look at Fred, quietly sipping his tea, dunking the last biscuit he'd managed to hide before the container was removed.

****

Evelyn Harwood had always seen Spirit. She knew no different. As far as she was concerned they were as much a part of this world as anyone else. That is until the day her mother took her to one side and said, "Darling, the little boy you say you play with is not really there."

"But he is Mummy, *look*, he's smiling at you."

Heartbreaking then to see her innocent little face collapse into tears as her mum gently explained that she was a very, very special girl, who could see and hear the people of the Magic Kingdom; but

16

if she told others about it they would laugh at her, and the magic would go away.

It wasn't until many years later that Evelyn allowed herself to work with Spirit. Having suppressed the gift she'd been born with. To be honest it made her day to day life much easier if she ignored the life-like apparitions and the voices in her head.

The wake-up call came from her mum. She'd only been dead a few days when she came through. It started with the heavy aroma of Chanel No 5; totally out of place in the kitchen, it completely masked the strong smell of garlic in the Spaghetti Bolognese.

At first Evelyn dismissed the sign. When the light above her head started to flash on and off like a Belesha beacon she *had* to take notice.

Emotions flooded her body as she mentally linked with the energy that could only have been her mum.

'*Sorry, I'm so sorry.*' Was the first communication. Swiftly followed by, '*I only did it to protect you; people don't understand a gift like yours. My mother had it. She was hounded like a witch; blamed for any catastrophe in the village.*

I love you Evey.'

"Mum. Mum. You haven't gone."

'*I'll never leave you. I'm free at last from my worn out body. But I'll always be near; just a thought away.*'

"But I miss you Mum. Please come back."

'*I can't come back darling. As much as I love and miss you, I don't really want to. I'm pain fr ee. I can move around with just a thought. And your dad met me.*'

"Oh Mum."

'*I can't keep the connection for much longer. The density of your earthly vibration is so heavy; such a strain on my energy. I'm only a novice, next time will be better .*'

"Please don't go Mum. *Please.*"

'*Remember Evey.* I'm *just a thought away; still your mum. I'll always love you.*'

She'd gone. The Chanel No 5 with her. But she was just a thought away. Still her mum.

"Thank you God." Evelyn softly said to the light that was no longer flickering.

"Thank you."

Chapter 4

"He's not a believer, is he?" Mrs. Harwood said as she welcomed her visitors.

I may look senile, well past my sell by date, but I can still spot a brick wall a mile away, she thought, slowly giving the three members of the Brooks family the visual interrogation.

The mother and daughter would be OK, but he'd be a challenge to God himself. Where there's no sense there's no feeling. How true. I don't mind anyone being unsure, asking questions. Let the message be the proof. I don't know what's worse, a closed mind, or a gullible one? Who said, 'You can't give enough proof to non believers, and true believers don't need proof.' I'm not sure I agree with either of those statements.

Standing there, shaking his head, thinking what he could do with the money his wife and daughter were wasting on the private sitting with the mad witch, Fred gave every indication of being a non believer; a man with a closed mind.

"Am I doing all of you?" Evelyn Harwood wanted to know.

"Ya certainly not doing *me*," Fred answered.

"Can you do both of us together?" Julia politely asked, Mum giving her own agreeing nod.

"Why not? Two for one. Just like at Morrison's." Evelyn beamed as she stroked a slender hand down the new cotton skirt.

Evelyn loved a bargain, like the skirt. She'd only treat herself to the tins of best red salmon when they were on the two for one offer. John West of course, like Mum would serve on special occasions.

"Ring me when you're finished. I'll just nip into town." Fred was halfway into the Focus by now.

Nip into *Ladbrokes* more like, Miriam thought.

The flat was small but clean. First impression; old fashioned but comfy, luxurious possessions obviously not a priority. The only signs of extravagance were a large Royal Crown Derby teapot and a beautifully ornate silver picture frame decorated with Angels. On closer inspection this contained a sepia coloured photo of a bride and groom.

"I can't make the loved ones come you know. They've got free will just the same as us." Mrs. Harwood forewarned them.

"Please try," Miriam softly pleaded.

Evelyn closed her eyes, sinking back into the leather armchair. A silence filled the room, expectant and at the same time a tad disturbing; neither Julia nor Miriam knew what to expect.

A few empty minutes later Evelyn opened her eyes, looked directly at Miriam and said, "There's a young man trying to come through. Full of it he is."

Miriam gazed at Julia in amazement.

"Slow down young man, there's no rush." Evelyn warned the communicator. "What did you say?" Evelyn stared into the emptiness before her. "His energy isn't very strong. I keep losing him. Take your time love, you're amongst friends. It sounds like Jamie or Emery. That's a funny name."

"It's my Jeremy." Miriam shouted, almost jumping from the settee. Julia helped her mum back to her seat.

"He says he left his body so quickly. First thing he was aware of was looking down at the wreckage. Look what he's done to my Jag, he keeps talking about the Jag. He seems more bothered about the car than his death." Evelyn pondered.

"Can I have a glass of water please?" Miriam said. "And Pet, pass me the handbag, I need a pill."

"Are you feeling alright Mrs. Brooks?" Evelyn's concern surfaced. "You've gone ever such a funny colour."

"I think my mother is allowed to go a funny colour after the evidence you've just produced out of fresh air." Julia sounded polite but firm, intending to make the medium fully understand Miriam's response.

Without taking offence, Evelyn said, "I only give what I get love. That's the first rule of medium-ship, and the most important."

"Is my son alright?" Miriam said between the tears.

"I'll go back and ask him love."

The manner in which Evelyn said this astounded Miriam. You'd think Jeremy was alive and well and sat there in the room instead of being dead and gone for nigh on a year.

Dead, the word still cut her to the core, the tranquilliser mercifully cushioning the blow.

"He says he loves it in the Summerland. No pains, no worries; no traffic jams. He misses the Jag. But no one needs transport where he is. Just think of a place and bingo, you're there."

"Ask him if he's met Grandma Brooks?" Miriam suggested.

"He says she was waiting in the tunnel of light; took him by the hand. He was baffled, couldn't understand how either of them had got there. Couldn't *accept* he was dead."

"That makes me feel so much better." Miriam relaxed: the beginnings of a smile softened her face. "Fred's mum spoiled him rotten. He was gutted and heartbroken when she died so suddenly from a massive heart attack. *DIED*. There, she'd finally said it, its sting duller, not nearly as sharp.

Julia's thinking: I knew Grandma Haslam wouldn't have met him at the Pearly Gates. Julia had to smile. *That* Grandma would be in the other place, evil woman that she was. The only reason Julia had gone to that funeral was out of respect for Mum.

"There was a little boy with Grandma, says he never

touched the earth plain, he belongs to one of you. He insists one of you should know him; calls himself Frederick." Evelyn continued. "Took hold of Jeremy's other hand."

"Thank you Mrs. Harwood. He's mine." Julia burst into tears.

Miriam pulled her distraught daughter close, stroking away the pain as only a mother can.

The tears over, Julia faced the medium, "I don't believe it." Only immediate family knew I had a miscarriage. Just Mum, myself, and my husband Harry knew it was a boy. We hadn't told Dad because he'd have been devastated. He always wanted a grandson. I was told it would be difficult for me to carry another. *And Frederick.* That was the name he would have carried."

At that moment Miriam was sure the Spirit World existed. *Was* real. Her enormous, unbearable weight of despair and loss began to diminish. She knew her son's physical body was gone. But the glorious confirmation, the evidence produced by this little old lady, this medium, Mrs. Harwood, proved, beyond a shadow of doubt that communication was indeed possible beyond the grave.

"Hallelujah praise the Lord." Miriam joyfully exclaimed. "Oh dear, I must sound like a member of the Gospel singing brigade." She looked at Julia and winked. "So what. I'm not bothered."

The medium's expression changed. "He's pulling away now. He's gone," the celestial connection with the Spirit World broken.

"Can we come again tomorrow?" an excited Miriam wanted to know. "Jeremy can share some memories with us. That would be nice Julia, wouldn't it?"

"It doesn't work like that my love." Evelyn started in, sounding a little placating. "He needed to get through. Even though he was weak, not at his full spiritual strength. It'll take time for him to adjust to the Summerland. You see he went before his time, not through natural causes. His essence, his spirit, his soul if you will, was catapulted from his body. The invisible silver chord attaching body to spirit was torn to shreds. He has to recover. It will take time. But he just had to let you know he was alright, and pain free. You know, love is such a powerful thing. It's *eternal*."

Chapter 5

"He'll have to build his strength up. Acclimatise to his new home; realise he's no longer burdened with the physical body. All physical pains have gone. Limitations of the body have gone. Just a thought and whoosh, there he is, any destination he desires."

Evelyn paused, allowed Miriam and Julia to digest all the information. Always good to give people time; it's a shock, the first proof positive of life after death. In her many years as a medium she'd helped numerous clients in their quest for confirmation, acceptance that loved ones actually *survived* the transition between this world and the next.

"He'll miss the Jag. He loved that car," Miriam exclaimed.

"I doubt that," Evelyn said quietly. Raising her voice she continued. "We're all on a wonderful journey. Thank *God*. Yes, let us thank God, The Lord, Allah, Jehovah, Buddha, whatever you want to call the All Seeing, All Knowing deity that is common to all religions. In truth there is but one, any name will do. We're destined to have many sojourns. This earthly path is the hardest, the most difficult. We endure many pains. Face many fears, real and imaginary; experience numerous trials and tribulations. Some are tested more than others, Miriam. There must be very good reasons why some are chosen to suffer more than others. Sadly, it's not for us to know the whys or the wherefores.

"Even *myself*, a confirmed Spiritualist, found it so difficult to accept Mum's passing. I still miss the physical hugs and kisses. Of course I do, always will; but I found a poem, in a women's mag. I found it inspirational. It helped me so much, it really did. I'll get you a copy if you wish."

Removing a folded sheet of paper from an old handbag resting on the chair arm Evelyn passed it to Miriam.

<u>Transition</u>

Take my hand for I am going, to a place I've never been,
I do not know the way at all, I hope it's warm and green.
I'm not sure of the distance, or how I will get there.
So as I've done these many times, ask for help, inside a prayer.
Forgive me if I hesitate, or if I start to cry.
I'll find it hard, to just let go, but promise I will try.
I've heard that at transition, all fear, and pain will end.
Then we're led into the light, by angels, that you send.
I only ask of you my God, that you will stand by me.
I'm weak and only human, please help me to break free.
And if you've time to do it, I ask with all my heart.
Please let my friends, and loved ones know, 'tis not the end,
but my new start.

"Pass me the tissues, Mum." Julia voiced between the sobs.

Miriam obliged, taking one to stem her own tears.

"Thanks so much for seeing us Mrs. Harwood. You *have* dulled my pains; Julia is obviously touched by the experience. I would indeed appreciate a copy of the poem, if you don't mind?"

"It will get easier, for both of you; but the emptiness will always be there. I took much more than just comfort from that poem, I took hope, without *hope*, life is so empty. Just remember that all things must pass, but that love *never* dies. Tell me Miriam have you ever thought of going to Church?"

Miriam shrugged, looked sheepish, as though she'd done wrong, "I er, stopped going when I was at school. Drifted away from it so to speak. Then I met Fred. Pretty soon we had a family, so regrettably no time for religion."

"No, please, you misunderstand my question. I meant the Spiritualist church."

"I paid a visit to Hasland a few months ago," Julia interrupted. "You were doing the demonstration."

"That must've been their Easter Festival Special, I always do that one for them."

"I'll tell you one thing Mrs Brooks," Evelyn stated earnestly, "you might not get a message from your lad, but you'll surely find some comfort there, in Church, amongst fellow sufferers, and mourners of course. They too are finding it difficult to cope, come to terms with the loss of loved ones. Just talking, perhaps sharing a few tears with someone who really knows how you feel, certainly will help. Yes. That's a promise"

****

"Wott time does this Church thing start?" Fred asked Miriam.

Miriam hung her pac- a- mac in the cloak room, it would soon dry out in the warmest room in the house. She always said the radiator installed by the heating engineer was too big; men and their silly ideas. She sat at the kitchen table opposite Fred, removed the latest fashion statement from her tortured feet and said, "That's better. Well, Julia says six thirty, but it's best to get there early. They only put out thirty seats. It was full when she arrived at twenty past; the fold up chairs kept for emergencies had to be dragged from the storeroom.

"We could have our tea early; it will be late when we get back."

"If our Julia can take ya, I can still have me tea at six." Fred suggested.

"Always thinking about your belly. Surely you can manage till I get home; shouldn't be any later than nine. I think you've enough fat reserves to sustain you till then."

"Now don't be sarci. It don't become ya. Ya know I like me meals at regular times." Fred got up from the table to put the kettle on, gagging for a brew. "And don't take it out on me cos them there new shoes are crippling ya."

"That's got nothing to do with it, don't change the subject. You could have the Spam sandwiches a bit later than usual; live dangerously for once. I'm sure your delicate metabolism will eventually recover."

Spam. She hated the bloody stuff. It was alright in the Seventies; times were harder then, shops had limited choices. Miriam suspected Fred only ate it because the Monty Python team did a silly sketch about it. She hated them as well. Funny ? I don't think so. I've laughed more giving birth, stitches included.

Fred *always* had Sunday tea at six. It was a ritual. Started when he was still at school. *The Lone Ranger* was on from five thirty till six. Yes, Kemo-Sabay. Hi Ho Silver, away, followed by half an hour of news before *What's my Line*.

Miriam recalled all of this. When married, in Pit Row, Fred had still liked to continue with the routine. Fred hated the news, not wishing to hear the latest celebrity scandals or terrible, disturbing reports from the war zones. She'd taken him for better or worse. A vow is a vow.

"Anything for a quiet life," she said. "I'll ring our Julia and ask her. She usually goes to Bingo on Sunday night but I'm sure she won't mind. She's not awkward like *some* people we know. Can you possibly make your own sandwiches, or should I plate them up for you?"

"Sarcasm is the lowest form of wit. I'm not helpless ya know".

"I've seen your sandwiches, Freddy Boy. Door stops more like. I'd have to dislocate my jaw like a boa constrictor to get one of *those* slabs in my mouth."

Fred wanted to say, 'Don't kid yourself.' He thought better of it.

Miriam jumped up from the table, nearly tripping over the high heeled shoes she'd placed under her chair. "I'll ring Julia now, while I think about it."

No problem. Julia would love to go to Hasland on Sunday.

Miriam offered to pay the petrol money.

"Don't be daft, Mam." Any payment deemed offensive. Besides, Julia wanted to see another demonstration of mediumship. She considered herself a total novice in Spiritual matters, said as much on the phone. She'd almost said *virgin*, but she knew Mum would have blushed at the word. Sex education was still very primitive in the early eighties, and Miriam, a shy and timid woman, found it awkward and embarrassing to describe the sexual bodily functions to her daughter. So Julia learned the old fashioned, time-honoured way most adolescents did. Usually behind the school bike shed or during secret bedroom research with her best friend Maureen - a much quicker learner with a natural rhythm and ability in the subject - proud mother of twins when only just sixteen.

"I'll miss the Bingo," she'd told Miriam on the phone. "But If I ask Harry nicely I'm sure he'll let me go on Tuesday instead."

Now Harry was getting to be just like her dad. He didn't like changes at all. Even the reproductive act could only be performed on certain days. In certain postures of course. The missionary position usually being executed on a Saturday night, after Match of the day. Depending on how Forest had performed the degree of sexual satisfaction was either good, bad, or indifferent. But always messy.

"I'll pick you up about five thirty," she'd told her Mum, "should give us plenty of time."

Chapter 6

"Good evening ladies, would you like any raffle tickets?"

Mrs. Roberts was on the door as usual, a ruddy faced bubbly woman who ambushed anyone entering her church. No one was spared.

"I know it only looks like a shed, but we worship the Lord here. It's a church in *His* eyes." Said almost by rote to all newcomers entering Hasland Spiritualist Church.

"We'll take two strips please," Miriam answered, paying the one pound donation to the church funds.

A broad smile and a cheery, "Please take a hymn book and sit where you please," made them less anxious. "There are no reserved seats here," Mrs. Roberts concluded, turning to the next victim, sorry, visitor.

Being early meant that Miriam and Julia had the pick of the room; almost. Four seats were taken at the front, regulars, Julia decided, guiding her mum to the back row, close to the wall.

By 6.25 all seats were taken.

Julia scanned the room, surprised at her findings. "Have you noticed Mum?" She whispered, "there's only a couple of men here, I wonder why?"

The regulars sat with their glasses of water. Average age, sixty plus. All smartly dressed, chatting away about the weather and how cold it was getting.

A white haired lady passed Julia two blue *Songs of Praise* books, well worn like their distributor. "The hymns tonight are twenty one and forty two," she informed the newcomers with a smile that said, 'Welcome, please come again.'

The room went quiet. Miriam and Julia stopped mid conversation, looking round for reasons for the abrupt silence.

"Thank you all for attending tonight's service. Mr. George Atkins will be our demonstrator. Please give him a warm Hasland welcome," the multi talented Mrs. Roberts announced from the rostrum.

The congregation managed a gentle applause.

"Mr. Atkins will open in prayer, please send him all your love." Mrs. Roberts prompted before standing to one side of the platform.

All heads bowed, awaiting the medium's words of wisdom.

Miriam began to relax, enjoying the peaceful atmosphere; she'd *never* call it a shed. Not respectful.

Mr. Atkins's words offered very sincere philosophy. His conclusions concerning the state of the World today were so valid: "There is a great need for more love and compassion to our fellow man. We are too selfish. We are destroying our planet."

The address over, the first hymn *How great thou art* resounded round the walls. Singing over, Mr. Atkins resumed his position at the rostrum, time now to demonstrate his medium-ship.

The validity of the evidence from the World of Spirit was questionable; vague and definitely ambiguous in places. Newcomers to the fold, like Miriam and Julia, wouldn't be impressed. The hymn book lady didn't understand the significance of a June anniversary as stated by Mr. Atkins.

"This gentleman I have with me insists you should know of a passing in June," the medium repeated.

"A *passing*?" It dawned on the woman. "Oh yes, my uncle Jim died in June. But that was many years ago. I thought you meant a birthday or something."

"It's still a celebration to them my love." Atkins proffered quietly, meaningfully. "Just as significant an occasion as their birth. And time has no relevance at all up there."

So really that's another yes, Julia noted, thinking of her own circumstances. She'd always remember Jeremy's departure from this world, November the 23rd 2006. A black day for the Brooks family. The blackest.

"This Atkins chap is very good, even though he's not much of a promotion figure for his namesake's diet; he must weigh at least twenty stones. I hope the platform's reinforced." Miriam repressed a giggle with difficulty as she whispered to her daughter.

Julia looked around the congregation, surprised that all the women were delving into their handbags. "They can't all be looking to repair their make-up," she said to Miriam, who was looking at the song book index to see if she knew any of the titles.

"Collection *please* Mr. Manston," Mrs. Roberts said to the tall wiry man who suddenly appeared in the aisle, a well worn circular bowl in his hands.

By the time Mr. Manston had passed the bowl down to Julia it was half full of coins.

"Fancy putting copper coins in," Miriam said to Julia.

"It *is* free will offerings at the Divine Service, it says so on the notice board," Julia replied. "All donations are welcome, meagre or not. They all add up you know."

The service ended with a pleasant hymn Miriam had never heard before, followed by the closing prayer. Atkins devoted this to healing our planet. Ending with his plea to all of us to respect the wonderful wildlife so often abused and taken for granted.

The raffle followed. No luck there. Then the *obligatory* tea and biscuits, and quite welcome too.

Julia munched her biscuit as she watched Mr. Atkins waddling down the aisle making a bee line for the refreshments table.

I bet he likes his biscuits by the packet, she thought.

Atkins, enjoying a *McVitie's* Wholemeal, stopped by them, introducing himself as George. "Excuse me darling, but you had a young male spirit standing behind yourself and the lady in the corner. But I couldn't get a link. The energy was too low." He sprayed Miriam with digestive crumbs.

Miriam brushed them off. "We, er, we were so hoping you would come to us with a message," she politely said to what she looked upon as a humanoid biscuit devouring machine.

"Perhaps next time, you never know." He said, promptly heading back for more refreshments.

Next time I'll bring you a bib. Miriam promised herself, wiping the rest of the crumbs from her best Jacques Vert jacket.

Mrs. Roberts placed her cup on the table and approached Julia, gave her a lovely warm hug. "It's *so* nice to see you again."

Julia was amazed that this lady had recognised her, must've been at least six months since the last visit, probably more.

"We urgently need new members. I can't tempt you and your friend can I?" Mrs. Roberts appealed.

"Well, we are friends, but this is actually my mum Miriam. What do you think Mum?"

"I'm tempted. What do you think?"

"I'm game if you are. It should be interesting."

"Then we'll have a go. What do we have to do Mrs. Roberts?"

Mrs. Roberts had the appearance of a demure pensioner but she took no prisoners when it came to church matters. She excelled in recruiting new blood.

"I'll just nip into the office, get you the forms to fill in; you can bring them back next week."

Chapter 7

"I don't believe it. You and our Julia becoming Spiritualists. Whatever next?"

Fred worried more about the severe disruption to his eating habits than the possibility of any harm coming to his wife and daughter by joining the ghost hunting brigade. He'd actually watched *Most Haunted* one night, just to see what the research team got up to. His opinion, '*A load of rubbish*. That hysterical woman wants a right good slap; does *me* head in. She'd win Olympic gold for squealing. Any spirits would *definitely* be scared away by her antics. Silly woman.'

His nearest and dearest arrived home absolutely full of it all; they didn't stop nattering. Fred tried to ignore the constant tittle-tattle by sticking his nose in the paper but found that he couldn't.

"Why don't you join, Dad? Become a Spiritualist." Julia ventured, sceptical about broaching the subject, bearing in mind his swift departure when he'd dropped them off at Mrs. Harwood's. "There's a real shortage of men in the church."

"That's because *we* got more sense."

"Mrs. Roberts says you need to be very sensitive to work with spirit," added Julia, looking to Miriam for support.

"Very *gullible* more like." Fred insisted. They wouldn't fool me. I'd see right through em."

Julia laughed, "no doubt you would Dad, Spirit are not solid matter."

****

Julia worked part-time at the local library, three mornings a week. Harry enjoyed a good position in the IT industry. At thirty he was the oldest employee in the office. His managerial salary meant that her wages could be used for luxuries such as holidays or new clothes; usually the latter.

The library was only a small one; attached to the youth club. Hardly worth keeping open with its membership of fifty. But the council deemed it a necessary expenditure; justifying it as being an oasis of learning in the former mining village. Most of the pits had closed years ago – the result of Maggie's anti-union holocaust and Arthur Scargill's destruction of the NUM. Between them they had done what two world wars failed to do; they'd brought British coal production to an all-time pathetic low, and eventually divided the mining community into two distinctly separate factions.

Unforgivable. Brother didn't talk to brother. Father fought with son; distraught mothers playing referee somewhere in between. Dad Fred was furious; he always blamed the Conservatives.

She'd miscarried at fourteen weeks. The boy would've been named Frederick Harry Brentnall. Dad would have liked that. Dad put on a hard face about most things but deep inside him was a real softy, and one easily hurt. A miner all his life influenced his actions to a great degree. It's a man's world down the pits. No room for petty deeds or silly words. A life could easily be lost in the dark cavernous depths. Trust and respect were paramount, both had to be earned the hard way.

When she'd lost Frederick Harry, knowing she might never carry a child again, Julia decided Dad couldn't be told. She knew it would have broken his heart.

Working in the library had its merits. The busiest day was Wednesday, when the Selston WI exchanged their Catherine Cookson's and Rosamund Pilcher's. With only six members left, all of them seventy plus, a rush hour it was not.

One day she mixed a few Jackie Collins and Danielle Steele titles in amongst the favourite fodder of the blue rinse brigade. It nearly caused a riot, the old biddies far from amused to the extent they declared such filth should be banned; removed from the library at once.

Mondays were a doddle. Usually occupied with copying menus from the vast array of cookery books in stock and catching up with any letters she might have to write.

The Monday after accepting the offer of membership of the Hasland Spiritualist Church Julia decided it would be a good time to improve her limited knowledge of the Spiritualist Religion and their beliefs.

Spiritualism and the Occult was showing as being in stock on the archaic Windows 98 driven laptop. Mum certainly wouldn't like any involvement with the occult. The very sound of it brought images of devil worship, sacrifices and witchcraft.

Actually, the book was a marriage of two subjects. Skipping the occult section Julia became absorbed in the section on :
Spritualism.

She was amazed at how long it had been in existence in this country. Having read somewhere about the famous Helen Duncan trial of 1944, she didn't realise that ten years later Spiritualism was officially accepted as a religion, just like any other. Mum would like that. With much to read she did find herself skimming through pages, hoping something would take her attention.

"Ah. There it is, Mediums and Psychics."

Julia absorbed what it said:

A medium is a sensitive person, male or female, generally female, who has the ability to connect with the Spirit World. They act as the go-between to deliver information to a living recipient.

Clairvoyance is the ability to see Spirit.

Clairaudience, the ability to hear Spirit.

Clairsentience, the ability to sense Spirit.

Clair knowing, the ability to know of the presence of Spirit.

"Wow, impressive stuff."

Julia hungrily thumbed through the pages until she located *Psychic*: the extra sensory ability to use the higher levels of the mind to pick up information from living things; more commonly called, the Sixth Sense.

"So that's how it works. I must borrow this book and show it to Mum."

****

"Don't let your Dad see it," Miriam warned. "He'll only make fun, ridicule it all. Bring it over here, we'll look together."

Julia was buzzing with information. "It's fascinating Mum.

There's sections on near death experiences, tarot cards." Moving closer to her mum on the settee she flipped pages, reciting many aspects of the craft. "There's auras, chakras, the lot. One thing's for certain, we sure have a lot to learn. If half of this is true, it offers a totally new view of why we are here, and what happens at death."

"But why haven't we heard of any of these things our Julia? It don't seem possible that most of mankind is oblivious to all this information."

"*Because*, although it's general knowledge and readily available if you look for it, meaning whoever looks for it. It's certainly not promoted, or even advertised. The only media coverage is done in a derogatory and biased manner. *Spiritualists* don't go knocking on doors on Sunday mornings trying to force their ideas on people with better things to do on their day off."

Miriam chuckled. Julia had triggered a distant memory. "They certainly picked the wrong house that Sabbath morning. Can you remember? Your dad was busy wo rking out his betting slips payout from Saturday's racing when they knocked on the door. Remember? I took you into the kitchen. The last straw was when the timid middle-aged woman with a hairstyle copied from the *Last of the Mohicans,* tried to tell Fred that gambling was a sin and he should abstain from any future temptations, repent immediately or suffer the consequences. You *must* remember the *haircut*.

"*Anyway*. He blasted off a tirade of expletives that I won't repeat. I daren't. Most of the words containing four letters, all naughty. *Anyway*. The woman and her male companion were totally shell shocked. They retreated down the path dropping Awake and Watchtower's everywhere. Somethin' I'll *never* forget, especially the haircut."

"You *must* remember Julia."

"Some of it." Julia was forced to chuckle at the look on Mam's face. "But certainly not as well as you."

Julia placed the book on the table, "Mum."

"Yes love."

"We are doing the right thing aren't we?"

"What do you mean?"

"Well, Jeremy's gone. We can't bring him back, can we?"

"No. Of *course* we can't. So?"

"Just a thought. Perhaps we should move on, forget him."

Miriam stared at Julia. "I can't move on as you put it. I need to know he's alright. Not in any pain or distress. I *can't* forget him. I *won't*."

They had a cry.

"Hey, Julia, I forgot to tell you, Mrs. Roberts rang to ask if we could make it on Sunday. A lady from Sheffield will be taking the service."

Chapter 8

Sunday, six o'clock.

Fred settled down to his tea. In Dad's treasured and very private property, this meant the Parker Knoll recliner. It was completely out of bounds to everyone. Except Pippa, the most beautiful pure bred Siamese cat on the whole planet. At least Fred thought so. She was far superior to mere mortals of course; fussing and petting allowed strictly on *her* terms. But she had a weakness for Fred, more so his father's Draylon covered armchair.

Miriam used to say Pippa only wanted to sit on the soft cushion; Fred was actually in the way. But he'd have none of that. The once mustard coloured chair was a bit worse for wear after all these years, but so was Fred.

'Waste not, want not,' was Dad's favourite saying. 'Look after the pennies and the pounds will look after themselves,' another gem.

Frederick Arthur Brooks senior had a lot of these archaic, timeless pieces of wisdom, waiting like a legacy to be passed down to his one and only heir, young Freddy.

Junior liked nothing more than four slices of thick brown bread, Hovis of course, filled with a generous amount of Spam. Followed by a dish of apple pie - Mum's secret recipe - drowning in a deluge of thick canary yellow custard.

The special recipe apple pie had gone, along with its creator, Mrs. Ethel Brooks, Freddie's doting Mum; but the Spam sandwiches lived on.

Miriam never understood any of it. To her it was a silly eccentric routine. She never did get on with his mum anyhow; too bossy by half in her opinion.

But every Sunday, at six o'clock, he relived the past, the good old days, when Mum and Dad took care of everything, especially Fred junior.

The *Lone Ranger* and *What's my Line* had long passed into history, along with both parents, but Fred stubbornly clung to the last vestige of nostalgia, the Spam sarnies. Julia had tried the

Spam, finding it too peppery for her taste. 'She never complains when she stuffs her face with that foreign 'Spaggy Bolly' concoction; all you can taste is the garlic. Them there Italians will never have a vampire problem.' Fred had commented at the time.

Fred's of the opinion they ought to bring the test card back, more entertaining than most of the rubbish served up at six.

He poured the ready-made custard over the Mr. Kipling individual Bramley apple pie and waited for the microwave to warm up his dessert. A poor substitute for Mum's, not only was the secret ingredient missing from the pie, eventually identified as ground nutmeg when he was sent to the corner shop at baking time, but the custard imposter lacked something. *Lumps.* That was it. Lumps somehow added a consistency, an improved taste. Yes, the home made variety was far better.

Nothing is the same. Bring back black and white tellies. Bring back *Billy Cotton's Band Show*. "*Wakey Wa-a-a-key*!" Now that was proper entertainment. Alan Breeze was crap, but Kathie Kay was a little darling.

As much as Fred moaned about the progress, or not, of household gadgets, he had to agree that the invention of the infra-red remote control was a real milestone, a paramount improvement over the primitive corded version.

Many a time he had almost tripped over the thin grey cable, buried in the long shag pile rug like a military trip-wire. The cat was nearly decapitated on more than one occasion. Bless her, in his own way, Fred really loved Pippananamorthy, her Siamese Cat Club registered name; quickly condensed by all the family to *Pippa*. Good idea, ya couldn't get ya gob around a name of that magnitude; she was only a cat after all.

Cat and human: their relationship didn't have a good beginning. From the day Miriam bought the blue-eyed kitten into the house it was obvious things would no longer be the same. With the addition of another female into the Brooks' residence Fred and Jeremy became the minority party; evermore to be outvoted in any debate. Soon proven by the necessity to replace the front room curtains; torn to shreds by the feline's constant climbing to the top rail, sliding down like a mountaineer who has lost her grip, frantically needing to save herself by clawing at anything in reach. The final decision as to colour and pattern of the new drapes was made by Pippa, growling in her deep, almost human, guttural voice when Miriam and Julia asked her if she liked the sample they were gently rubbing across her nose. Fred told them they should be rubbing her talons with it, receiving the inevitable and definitely unanimous, "Shut up Fred," from wife and daughter, accompanied by a supportive growl from the cat.

The good old days. Nostalgia Land is wonderful, memories make events seem bigger; always better.

Nearly always better.

A flash from the past invaded his thoughts. Unwelcome, uninvited, disturbing. He had to acknowledge the intruder. Reluctantly.

Fred's introduction to Miriam's parents was the offending flash back.

The Haslam's lived in a big house, at the top of Albert Street, the posh area of the predominantly mining village. Mr Haslam had opened the door. "Welcome young man. Are you taking my daughter out?" A smile and a handshake followed.

"If ya don't mind sir," Fred had replied, in awe of the location and size of the property.

"Well come in lad, don't just stand there."

Miriam's dad offered Fred a seat in the hallway. "She won't be long, just gone to change her shoes. Says they don't match her skirt. Funny things women, don't you think so lad?" He winked.

Fred remembered that he'd just smiled, shrugged his shoulders in an awkward way, what did a young lad like him know of women?

Miriam soon joined Fred in the hallway, kissed her dad and asked him to leave the door unlocked.

Fred could hear the words now, "Be home by ten mind you. Or I'll come looking for you." Mr Haslam stood prominent in the doorway, like a sentry.

"Have ya a *mam*? Ya never talk about a mam." Fred queried,

escorting his first girlfriend down the drive, destination The Odeon cinema.

"Only on paper, she *hates* me. Blames *me* for my brother's death. As if *I* had anything to do with it. Dad is all I've got. He's wonderful. *There* she is, looking through the upstairs curtains."

Silly cow, Fred remembered thinking of the furtive Mrs. Haslam.

"Mum's friend Dorothy, ya know, her baby died. Went to Jesus." Fred comforted Miriam by squeezing her hand. "But on Resurrection Day we'll all come back. *Mum* says so, it's in the Bible."

The reminiscence had been sustained long enough. Too long. Mrs. Haslam memories troubled Fred to this very day.

Wrenching away from the mental torment he picked up the plate and mug used for his tea, washed them in the sink, dried them, putting both items back in the cabinet. "Who needs a dishwasher?" He sneered at the stainless steel model gleaming back at him.

Returning to the Parker Knoll he released the leg support, slumped into the cushions and closed his eyes.

Just time for a quick nod before Nigella gets back.

Pippa jumped up, did a few circuits of Fred's lap then settled with her head hanging over his knees. Within minutes both were asleep.

Chapter 9

Mrs. Ruth Simmons from Sheffield didn't go down too well. Even Miriam, a new recruit to the Spiritualist movement, didn't feel much if any proof had been presented by the medium that she was indeed communicating with Spirit forces. The only positive feedback came from Mrs. Barrows, a long term resident of the Victoria Road Care Home, described by Mrs. Roberts as 'a silly nuisance who only came for the refreshments.'

"It would help if her hearing aid worked; it's always acting up. She'd say yes if you asked if her name was Robbie Williams." This was whispered by Mrs. Roberts to Miriam, just in case the temperamental hearing aid was functioning. "And as for that Simmons woman, she only works on a psychic link, plays the averages. It's obvious."

"What do you mean 'plays the averages'?" Miriam questioned.

"I've been a member of the SNU, that's the Spiritualist National Union to you my dear, for almost forty years; I could do better than her. But *I* know my limitations; I'm a healer and proud of it. A *medium* I'm not. Whenever I see a demonstration like tonight's it really makes me angry.

"She deludes herself that woman. Worse than that, she's tarnishing the genuineness of our movement. Doing Spirit a total injustice. It's so easy to deceive people. Tell them what they want to hear."

Miriam frowned. "I don't understand what you mean?"

"Well, let's say I go to a woman like you. You're mid-sixties, right?"

"Sixty-four actually, but I haven't put any make up on tonight."

"Anyway, it's close enough." Mrs. Roberts continued with a dismissive shrug. "So it's pretty safe to say that at least one, if not both of your grandmas are dead."

A nod.

"Now, if I said I was linking with a small, frail looking old lady, who came with a lot of love, you might be thinking I was in contact with your own grandma's spirit."

42

Another nod.

"I then might add she baked on a Tuesday."

"That's *amazing*. Grandma Haslam was very petite, five foot at most, very slightly built. And she baked bread every Tuesday and Friday. I looked forward to the fresh baked loaves she brought round, still warm; I can taste them now. How did you know that?"

"Not quite so amazing, or clever as you may think. In Grandma's day there was a lot of malnutrition in the working class; badly affecting pregnancies for years to come. These smaller babies grew up to be smaller adults. Especially the women, they were labelled as second class citizens until 1928 when they won the right to vote."

"Yes but you said that Granma Haslam baked on a Tuesday. How could you possibly know that?" Miriam looked flustered. And impatient.

"My dear," said Mrs. Roberts, "it's because most working class married women with a family had to bake their own bread. Monday was always washday, Tuesday became fresh bread day."

Miriam sighed, quite happy with the explanation. "The way you put it makes so much sense. I honestly thought you had Granma's Spirit with you. She was nice to me, like a mother." Miriam went quiet.

"I was just playing the averages my love. Nothing specific was ever mentioned. Credibility comes with the personal facts. Names, dates, places; relevant only to you."

"I can see where you're coming from now Mrs. Roberts; but golly, you sure had me going for a minute."

"Some people are so gullible. They accept almost anything from the medium, making it fit their own requirements. Some are so desperate they eagerly feed the medium. Most without realising it."

"*Feed* them, what, like sandwiches?" Miriam questioned the information.

"Almost. They feed them with facts and figures, given innocently, of course, without any qualms or hesitation. The medium merely fills in the gaps strategically left in the supposed

Spirit message."

"But I was convinced that Mrs. Harwood was with my Jeremy. That she was in contact with the other side."

"Oh *she* was; Evelyn is the real thing. She's no need to play the averages; her link with the Spirit world is truly awesome."

"Thank God for that. Just the thought that she was actually communicating with Jeremy was such a comfort. It gave me real hope for the future."

"We all need hope my dear. It's the only thing that keeps some of us going. When Ted passed even I struggled. It's one thing preaching to people that life is eternal and there is no death but when you actually lose someone, that's when you're tested. After the cremation it finally hit me that he'd gone. I only had to look at the old wooden walking stick in the porch and I'd sob my eyes out. The flesh is weak. Made even me question my faith."

"How did you cope then? *I* relied on tranquillisers."

"It was ever so funny really. Weird funny. Evelyn Harwood rang me to confirm she was still doing the service for us, she *knew* straight away something was wrong. I told her Ted had passed away. Oh she was such a help. That woman is a living Saint. She mailed me a lovely poem. I read it all the time. I can't tell you how much better it makes me feel reading those words."

"She said it helped when she lost her mum. It's in my handbag, you can read it if you want."

The poem was passed to Miriam. She settled down to read it quietly, indeed to absorb some of the comfort the other woman had hinted at.

Last night

**I thought I heard a voice last night, as I settled down to sleep.
It sounded like my mother, I sat up, and I did weep.
The reason for my show of tears, is my mother's dead and gone.
She passed away quite suddenly, it's dark where once she**

shone.
I never got the chance to tell, how much I loved her so.
I used to tell her in my head, I thought that she would know.
It's many years since we lost her, I think of her each day.
I ask God to be good to her, when I kneel me down to pray.
Jesus wants me for a sunbeam, was her favourite song of praise.
Every time she heard it, her spirits it would raise.
I must confess I took it bad, when she left us all so quick.
I could not grieve as others did, felt empty, always sick.
One day I began to know, it was time to show my love.
I cried and cried for hours, asked for help from Him above.
I now believe in eternal life, that the soul goes on and on.
For last night my mum did call, to prove she hasn't gone.

"She sent me another one called *Transition*; where does she get them from? How does she know which poem to send? They don't print such inspirational stuff in Fred's daily paper?"

"I know exactly what you mean; I stopped believing in luck and fate years ago. I'm sure things happen for a reason, at a pre-destined time. We mortals are only allowed to see the next step on our earthly path. The whole picture would probably blow our little minds." Mrs. Roberts touched Miriam's shoulder, continuing.

"Special people, like Evelyn, are more in tune with the higher realms, know a great deal more; their cosmic magnets for attracting wisdom. Nothing to do with their intellect."

"I agree with you," Julia butted in, she is a Saint. Mum is much better off reading the poem than taking the drugs."

Discussion over, Mrs. Roberts gave Miriam a huge smile. "*Anyway*, I've got news that might interest you. Come into the committee room, I'll tell you all about it."

"Can Julia come as well?"

"Of course she can. You're both fully paid up members."

****

Hasland Spiritualist Church was one of the smallest affiliated members of the SNU. Small in size, membership, and the elected hierarchy forming the committee.

If Mrs. Roberts, Annie to her friends, hadn't agreed with the President, Mrs. Clarke's request to fill in as the secretary, unpaid of course, as all officials are, the minimum acceptable Quorum wouldn't be met, and the governing body of the UK's Spiritualist Churches would be very displeased. A situation that could seriously jeopardize any future support; possibly resulting in the enforced closure of the church.

"My Ted always said you should never volunteer for *owt*." Annie grumbled. "As secretary I have to do all the bookings, chase up the Mediums, do the banking, paying out, and loads of other jobs."

The committee room was really a broom cupboard with a bench, separated from the kitchen with a B&Q matchbox construction type door. The words, 'Private authorized personnel only' roughly stenciled in red letters one inch high.

A bench filled the entire back wall. Solidly built in pine, it could comfortably seat four people. But *not* in today's company. Miriam looked at the space remaining after Julia sat down, then glanced at Annie. She had never really scrutinised Annie. Oh she'd seen her in the butcher's shop many times, but always from behind the serving counter. She'd casually noticed her outside the church, welcoming the congregation to the service. But she'd never seen Annie close up, and certainly not in a broom cupboard.

It looked like her normal size 14 upper half had been grafted on at the waist with the hindquarters of a prize Aberdeen Angus bull. The only thing Miriam could think of was that scene in *Jaws* where Roy Scheider, seeing the great white shark for the first time, turns to Richard Dreyfuss and says, 'We need a bigger boat.'

Annie remained standing. "Miss Barnes, she's the Vice President, suggested at the last Committee meeting that we should start an open circle."

"What's a circle?" Julia, quiet and content to listen until now, leaned forward to ask Annie.

Annie explained, "An open circle is where people with interest in the mysteries surrounding life after death get together to find the truth, hopefully some of the answers we all seek.

"It's run under the control and guidance of a medium. If any of the circle have talent and the dedication needed it can then be nurtured and moulded in a development circle, hopefully to a level making them worthy pioneers for Spirit; culminating in the ability to stand on the Church rostrum, demonstrating the awesome wonder of communication with the higher realms. Just like Evelyn Harwood."

Both Miriam and Julia looked gob-smacked at hearing this; such an intense promise of an awakening to the mysteries of life and death was hard to accept, even digest. A silent agreement to ask more later on passed between them.

"Miss Barnes says with the poor standard of some of the speakers we're getting, Mrs. Simmons from Sheffield being a prime example, we could do better ourselves."

"Oh...oh right." Miriam hesitantly nodded, looking to Julia for back up.

"So I'm going to approach Miss Dolly Jameson," Annie continued, "to see if she'll dedicate one night a week to run our circle. I met her last year at Stansted. She's a new demonstrator on the circuit, but I've heard some good reports of her platform work. She lives nearby, somewhere in Alfreton."

The committee had already voted, decision made. The initial open circle would run for eight weeks. With a maximum seven students. This would be time enough to reveal the people with the raw latent ability, dedication and interest. After a suitable break a development circle could then be considered; finer details to be confirmed as soon as possible.

"What about it Mum?" Julia wanted to know. "Are you up for it; I'm certainly interested?"

"I will if you will."

"That makes three of us then," Annie said, "only four more to go."

Dolly Jameson certainly was the new kid on the block. Only twenty two, but with impressive feedback from churches already served. Almost six feet tall, barely eight stone wet through; she could easily have passed for a stick insect. Sharp featured face, protruding golf ball eyes. And, to top this, poor girl, she suffered with an overactive thyroid gland, responsible for the excessive amount of facial hair exploding from her top lip. When she admitted to being an active member of Newton Spiritualist Church that was it. Work colleagues in the Alfreton branch of Boots the Chemist unkindly labelled her '*The Praying Mantis.*'

She knew of the nickname; not openly used in her presence. Not because her new workmates were sensitive to her feelings. Oh no. But because, in their ignorance, they associated witchcraft, spells and curses with the ability to talk to the dead, as they put it, and didn't want to take the risk of eternal damnation. Or being turned into a frog.

Dolly's Grandma Aggie had introduced her to the Spiritualist religion. Aggie lived and breathed the life of a Spiritualist. Always a shoulder to cry on, a listening ear, or just someone to ask for down to earth, common sense advice. The Sunday night ritual started as just somewhere to go, a bit of a lark really, the eighteen-year old Dolly taking to it like a duck to water. After four years of circles, workshops, and two intensive courses at the Arthur Findley College Stansted, she was recognized, and accepted, as the genuine article. A true bone fide Medium.

"Don't let it go to your head gel, remember *who* you're working for," Aggie impressed upon her, "the *Lord* giveth and the *Lord* taketh away."

"I wish he'd take my hairy lip and thyroid problem away," Dolly shot back.

"Be respectful child, beauty is only skin deep."

"Tell that to the horny male population of Alfreton, it might get me a date," she chelped.

Aggie bristled at that. "Sex, sex, sex, that's all you youngsters think about nowadays."

"The first one would do *me* fine Grandma. I think all three would kill me with ecstasy."

"Wash your *mouth* out young madam, it *doesn't* become you."

Aggie had made her point. The result being that Dolly would serve any church that invited her to take the service. Big or small, near or far, it didn't matter; she only asked for enough expenses to cover petrol money and a little extra for the wear and tear on her VW Polo. She'd worked in Kirton with a mere six people in the audience, and Sheffield with over sixty, so size didn't matter. She was working for Spirit. In Dolly's opinion to see the effects communications with the other side had on the loved ones left behind was priceless.

When Mrs. Roberts asked Dolly to take charge of the circle, it confirmed all the work and dedication had indeed been worthwhile. Dolly accepted with thanks.

Chapter 10

"I *knew* I should have kept my mouth shut. Mum always said you were selfish."

"She never did like me." Fred defended himself against Miriam's barrage.

Miriam was beside herself, what with Fred's attitude and all towards what she wanted to do. Upright and defiant in her easy chair an onlooker could see the flames leaping out of her eyes, hear the cogs in her head whirring a she bolstered herself to let fly with a few choice home truths.

"She had you weighed up alright. Used to say things like 'his eyes are too close together,' and, 'I'm sure he wipes his arse with that cap of his; stinks to high heaven. He's not coming into my house.' *That's* what she always said."

"Don't sit there quoting ya mother to me. Ya never liked her anyway. Besides, I was only expressing me opinion, woman." Fred physically retreated, his antagonism towards Miriam's new interest in the Spiritualist religion controlled; he didn't like the vitriolic response it had brought upon him.

"Ya can go if you like." Anything for a quiet life he decided, as not a wise decision to object to, or even criticise, his wife and daughter becoming part of the Hasland coven. "And just to correct ya, *Morticia*, that cap was me dad's, and I washed it in sink every Sunday."

"What in? *Cat piss?* And less of the Morticia or I'll get Mrs. Harwood to put a spell on you, turn you into a jack ass. Oh! I'm sorry, it's too late."

Miriam was really warming to the argument. Enjoying the power of attack. The meekest and most gentle person normally, but get this lady's back up at your peril.

She'd once proved her worth as a verbal heavyweight in Asda. The young male assistant kept insisting she'd only given him a ten pound note. She knew it was a twenty. The hole in the wall had just spat out five of them. It was all she had on her.

"Look! I've got eighty pound in my purse," she stated

adamantly. "Here's the slip to prove that only ten minutes ago I withdrew a hundred from the ATM outside. You've made a mistake."

"Madam, it was a *ten* pound note," the teenage moron parried with a smirk.

"Ring for your supervisor immediately," Miriam demanded through clenched teeth.

The matter was soon resolved. The duty manager had bustled up to investigate the commotion at till seven, wearing a smile obviously rehearsed countless times when dealing with complaints. A man who subscribed to 'the customer is always right' school. He opened the till, concluding that as the first twenty pound note in the tray perfectly matched the mint condition ones in Miriam's purse and numerically slotted into the sequence formed by the other four, then as far as he was concerned the case was proven. A genuine mistake had been made. He gracefully handed over the disputed change.

"Very sorry madam, it won't happen again."

"*Little liar*," she vehemently snarled at the now po-faced idiot being replaced on the till. He would've pocketed that tenner," she told Fred, who'd witnessed the altercation from his position by the Lottery kiosk.

Recollection over Miriam returned to the task in hand, Fred; addressing same with new vigour.

"The Hasland thingy's only for six weeks. Julia says *she'll* sacrifice her Tuesday night Bingo. Harry is agreeable. It's just *you,* misery guts." The torrent continued.

Fred slowly raised his eyebrows, thinking, how much longer is she *gonna* go on.

"Miriam darlin', ya know ya can go anywhere, anytime. I've no problems on that score. But there's a lot of charlatans about; I don't want ya to get hurt."

"Well why not come and join us? You can protect us all"

"Only if it starts after seven, I can't miss me tea."

On the tip of her tongue to say more, either that or hit him with the bloody chip pan, Miriam fell silent. She brooded.

"Cup of tea love?" Fred asked, his solution to all problems.

Miriam didn't acknowledge the surrender. Picking up the remote control she selected UK Living. Celebrity Masterchef, she would indulge in her triumph.

Chapter 11

Dolly's circle of six students was officially inaugurated on Tuesday the 13th of November. It could have been scheduled for the week previous, but Dolly wisely said it wasn't a good idea. "A lot of idiots will still be polluting the atmosphere with fireworks. The bangs and screeching noises won't be conducive to the serenity required for the circle."

It was the first time they'd met as a group. Seven chairs were set up in a circle at the front of the church, close to the rostrum.

Miriam and Julia sat either side of Dolly; Annie Roberts next to Miriam, then Summer, a lovely vision of youth and enthusiasm. Miss Doris Barnes, Vice president and spinster of the parish, sat by Julia. The final, not entirely willing member, was Fred.

"I don't believe it, surrounded by women." He wore a smug grin.

After this statement, what else, they all addressed him as Victor.

"We start at seven fifteen *precisely*," Dolly informed them. "The doors will be locked to keep out any unwanted visits from the local yob brigade. We should all blend together, respect each other's views and opinions, or it will not work," Dolly looked at each of the faces surrounding her, seeking response.

At least she knew Annie and Doris. The others were total strangers. None more stranger than Fred who sat there with arms crossed, flat cap at his feet.

He'll be a challenge, so what, he just might surprise us all.

"Right then everybody, it's time, let's start shall we?" The friendly chatter stopped and all eyes looked to Dolly for guidance.

"First thing, we always open in prayer. As this is your first week I'll do it. Next week I'd like Miriam to open. Then go round the circle, each one in turn."

Six blank faces trembled in unison.

"It sounds much harder than it really is," Dolly said, flashing a genuine warm smile. "I'd like you all to sit comfortably. No crossed legs or arms." She gave Fred a melting stare. "Close your eyes. Try to calm your body and mind. Respect where you are, who you are, and above all else, what we are attempting to do. Communicate with the Spirit World."

That said Dolly went into the prayer.

"Lord and father of all humanity, divine spirits and keepers of the higher realms, please watch over this circle of friends. We seek the truth, the evidence of life eternal.

"We ask that you protect us, surround us with the glorious shield of white light, allow us to blend our physical energies with the higher world's energies. Prove to one and all that there is no death, merely a transition, a shedding of the physical burden we call life. We ask all of this in the name of love and place ourselves in your care and keeping. Amen."

'Amen' was repeated by all the students, including Fred, who somehow looked calmer, more at ease than when he entered.

Dolly went on to explain, "At this stage we'll always go into meditation. That's a fancy term for deep relaxation. Everybody can do it. We all do it automatically every night. The difference here is that you *won't* fall asleep. You'll stay a fraction of energy away from the unconscious level we know as sleep. If you do fall asleep, don't worry, you'll be safe; I'll wake you up. Fifteen minutes will be plenty of time tonight. Don't be frightened, give it a chance; see what happens.

"Close your eyes, relax. I will now talk you through the first stage. Then just enjoy the peace and quiet until it's time for your return."

Miriam quickly looked at Fred, surprised he actually appeared to be getting involved in the exercise. He'd closed his eyes, hands resting on his thighs.

Julia responded like her mother; after a quick peek she settled down as instructed.

"We're going on a journey," Dolly intoned. "A special magical excursion into the inner world of the soul, where all things are possible. Pain and fear do not exist. Anger and stress are not an issue. All the answers you are seeking are there to be found. There are no limitations to your ability. No restrictions. No judgments made on age or worth. You are truly in control. Completely protected and safe.

"You're now feeling much calmer. More relaxed. Your breathing is becoming slower, less defined. All tension is leaving your neck; shoulders are lowering, released from the iron grip of stress. Negative thoughts and energies are leaving your body; absorbed by the earth. Feel the calmness. Stillness. Peace that is truly you. The essence; the seed of life. One part of the collective being."

Dolly gently opened her eyes to see how the group were reacting to their first guided meditation. To her relief, and surprise, all had their eyes closed, appearing to have responded to the talk down. Even 'Victor', bless him, was trying. Relaxed in face and body, both hands placed nicely on his thighs. His fingers gave him away, perched like talons on his knee caps, like a last hold on reality.

"You're now in the zone," Dolly advised softly. "The peace, the stillness, enfolds you. Use this brief time to replenish your life force. Absorb the serene ambience. Immerse yourself in the tranquillity. All things are possible. You are now in the energy field of Spirit. Receptive to their communications, or not. It's your choice. Your free will. They too have the same options.

"There are no obligations. Enjoy the moment. You're in control. Well protected. Feel the calm. Feel the peace. *Feel the silence*."

Dolly looked at the six members of the first ever Hasland circle. Miriam, Julia and Annie were nicely in the zone. Completely still in body, gentle flickering of the eyes perceptible beneath closed lids. Doris was trying, perhaps a little too hard, the effort mirrored on her taught face. It never works.

'Victor' will be all right.

Fred/Victor's fingers had released their death grip, his chin now rested on his chest.

A couple of more sessions and I think he'll surprise us all.

Dolly was content.

The revelation was Summer. The serenity of Spirit completely masked her youthful features. She was calmness personified, without any perceptible movements to indicate that she was actually alive and breathing. She'd the appearance of a perfectly formed statue, spoiled only by the rapid eye movements in danger of bursting from her long blue painted eyelashes.

Next time, Dolly decided, I'll ask Annie to change places with Doris. That should help to build the energy field around Fred.

The large wall clock over the entrance door was purposely positioned to help the medium taking the service regulate their demonstration. It now indicated the fifteen minutes allocated for the meditation had passed.

Dolly softly started the *'bring them back'* process

"It's now time to start your journey home. If anyone is with you, make your farewells, thank them for their company. Bring with you the positive, loving energy you've been surrounded with. Slowly draw away. Begin to raise your vibrations. Become more aware of your physical senses. Slowly *feel* the energy increase, as if awakening from a wonderful dream. But you will know it wasn't a dream. You were in that special place. Your innermost being, the essence that is truly you. You can return to it anytime, seek the company of the Spirit world, find the comfort of inner peace, replenish your soul strength."

Dolly monitored each of the group's responses to the gentle awakening call. All seemed well. No one had opened their eyes yet, she continued.

"Slowly feel the vibrations increase. You're now becoming aware of your physical body."

"You feel so good. So relaxed. So healthy. So uplifted. So positive. You're now fully united, soul and body; becoming aware of your breathing; soft, effortless. Slowly and gently open your eyes. Calmly accept your surroundings. You're home. Back with your friends, fellow travellers; united in the search for self and Spirit."

The first person fully alert was Doris. This didn't surprise Dolly one bit. Tries too hard that one. She may be the Vice President but she's the least sensitive person present.

The rest of the group came back within a few seconds of each other. *Except Summer.*

If Fred hadn't knocked her leg as he pulled the handkerchief from his trouser pocket she'd have remained in the semi-trance state.

Dolly wasn't too happy, apprehensive. I'll have to watch Summer, she goes very deep. If she can control the energies she'll be wonderful. If she wants to of course, she's very young. Actually she reminds me of myself at that age. *Awesome.*

Dolly became serious. "Now tell me, what did you all think of that exercise?"

"Did I snore?" Fred sheepishly asked, wiping his eyes.

"No," giggled Miriam, "*Why*? Did you fall asleep?"

Fred wriggled on his chair. "I'm not sure what happened. I did feel uncomfortable, a bit out of place to start with. Ya know, being the only man. I must admit I do have some reservations about this Spirit thing. But then I started to go with the flow, as you might say. I couldn't help meself. The calmness…. Well, it like engulfed me. The feeling of contentment was unbelievable. *Magic.* I actually felt my shoulders droop and all the tense muscles relax. Great stuff."

"Did you meet any Spirits? Or see any images?" Dolly asked, pulling a note pad from her handbag.

"I'm not sure what you mean by *see*. I had this impression of colours, like clouds moving about in me head. *Weird*."

"That's a terrific start Fred." She'd decided it wasn't really nice or polite to call him 'Victor'. The man was at least genuine, completely honest in his actions.

"Colours are very significant. They could be generated by your brain as a soothing influence of course, but it could also be Spirit energy. Did anyone else see colours?"

Julia and her mum both said they witnessed marvellous displays of colours. Vivid, sometimes swirling; yellows, blues, purples, and the purest, almost incandescent white.

"The actual colour can mean anything really," Dolly explained. "Purple, or amethyst to the colour chart brigade, means Spirit is around. Yellow, or gold, means healing forces. But these are only my interpretations. It's the same with symbols. A black cat to me means good luck. But if you've had a bad experience with a black cat you might think otherwise. We'll discuss symbols another day."

"I saw lots of angels and fairies dancing around a beautiful light," Doris said triumphantly, hands waving in the air.

You would. Dolly thought. There's always one.

Annie hadn't seen anything, saying the peace and comfort she'd experienced was enough. "I'll be pleased if I only get that. *Truly*. I came back feeling rejuvenated."

"Summer, how about you?" Dolly knew she'd saved the best for last, and wondered just how deep this teenager had really gone.

Summer offered a shy smile. "I saw the darkness first. Then it gradually became lighter, and lighter until it was almost too bright. Then I saw – well, I suppose they were *people*. I couldn't see the details; *far too bright*. They moved around, floated around… like feathers in a breeze. I just stared at them, hypnotized by the psychedelic display. I could have stayed there forever." The smile surfaced, this time more intently as if she had discovered inner peace. "Then suddenly, I was awake. It was … *fabulocious*."

There's a word I haven't heard before, mused Dolly. Must make a note of it, might use it one day. "You were almost in trance. Spirit surrounded you. But you have to be careful. *Remember,* you must be in control, always in control. It can be alarming and dangerous if things get out of hand. But that was wonderful. I'm really pleased. I'll give you the benefit of my knowledge and experiences. In time, you'll be able to use whatever gift you have for the advancement of Spirit awareness.

Dolly looked around her flock of future mediums, healers, philosophers, clasped her hands, smiled.

"We've done enough for tonight, I'll close in prayer."

Everyone settled, automatically closing their eyes in anticipation and respect.

"We give thanks to the Spirit world and our father God, for watching over us, for being part of this assembly of friends;

58

seekers of truth, proof of life eternal. I ask for a blessing on each head bowed before you. Guard and protect us until we meet again. All in the name of love. Amen."

The prayer over, everyone opened their eyes, shuffling and chair moving changing the atmosphere in an instant.

"I hope you all enjoyed your first circle," Dolly said, "and that you'll all come back next week. Oh yes, can you bring a pen and paper please? I'm hoping you'll all need them.

"Good night, have a safe journey home."

Chapter 12

"Are you pleased we pushed you into the circle Dad?"

Fred put his paper down, looked up at his daughter. "I'd have been happier with free membership, Spiritual enlightenment should be free; like prescriptions."

"Church rules say you have to be a member," Julia said, "I don't think five pounds a year is bad. Just think of it as another losing bet."

"He's got to have a moan," Miriam shouted from the kitchen. "Put the kettle on Julia, we'll have a nice cup of tea. It's a pity we couldn't use the church facilities."

"Dad, did you enjoy the meditation?" Julia asked, picking the tea pot up in readiness. "Dolly seemed to be happy with your progress."

"I have ta say I wasn't expecting anything at all. I thought it was all rubbish, mumbo jumbo stuff, served up for the gullible and desperate brigade. I admit I might be wrong. *Might be*, we'll see what happens." Fred poured the milk into the china cups, another archaic ritual, milk first then tea, always.

"There's hope for you yet. Next year you could be taking the service at Hasland." Miriam joked, winking at Julia.

"You're being sarci again; lowest form of wit ya know."

"I'm only kidding Fred. To be honest, Julia and I are proud of you. We know you only joined to protect us. But you were respectful, you gave the circle a fair chance to prove its worth; and you didn't snore."

"I was almost asleep ya know. Time just flew by. I didn't understand the moving, mist like clouds in me head. But so what, I felt happy and contented. I'll settle for that."

"I really wanted more," confessed Miriam.

"I know what you mean Mum, I did too. I was praying that

Jeremy would magically appear in my head. Stupid really."

For a few minutes the Brooks family just sat; cradling their cups and silently consoling each other.

Pippa jumped onto Fred's lap, almost knocking the tea cup out of his hand.

"Good job it were empty Dad, I bet she wants feeding." Julia said with a grin.

"She wants her claws cutting, she almost fetched blood that time." Fred winced, quickly placing his cup on the coffee table with one hand whilst clumsily discharging the aging feline assassin with the other.

Miriam's attention brought back to the real world she yawned; "Time for bed, Julia, let yourself out when you've done talking to your dad."

Julia tried her best. Despite the tender persuasion, and added inducement of a second cup of tea, Fred declined the offer of joining his wife and daughter at the next Sunday service. He was certainly becoming interested in the Spiritualist movement, but in no hurry to join them, more *proof* was needed. It would take time to wean him away from his habits, his comfort zone.

****

Miriam and Julia arrived early enough to secure the same seats as on their previous visit, eagerly awaiting more proof from the Spirit World.

Minister Jim Higgins from Burton on Trent was taking the service. He was, according to his CV, '*A very competent and confident communicator.*' His most impressive testimonial being from the Mecca of Spiritualism, The Arthur Findlay College, known to the initiated as Stansted.

In Annie Roberts opinion this was the country's finest College of Spiritual Education, attracting the best tutors in the world.

The library was famous for its huge collection of rare books, many with qualified testaments to the existence of spirit. The museum of artefacts was also an attraction not to be missed if you were lucky enough to visit the place.

Annie had been on one occasion, an open day the previous year, the quality of the demonstrations being so impressive she'd decided anyone who'd worked at the College would be welcome at her church.

Competent and confident he certainly was. What the CV didn't mention was that he was also boring. His slow, staccato pronunciation could've been tolerated if he'd given an interesting piece of philosophy, or any proof of Spiritual awareness. He struggled on both counts. He liked to hear himself talk; rambling on and on about his childhood in Mansfield; how he'd become a Minister of the SNU.

Annie, yet again nominated as chairperson, endured half an hour of tepid biography then decided enough was enough. "You only have ten minutes of the service left Mr. Higgins," she diplomatically informed him. "Could you try to connect with the Spirit realms and demonstrate your medium-ship *please*."

He carefully adjusted the SNU medallion hung ceremoniously round his neck, took a deep breath, then looked around the room for inspiration.

The first '*Spirit*' contact was acknowledged by Mrs. Barrows. She said yes to everything Jim threw at her. An old man who passed with cancer, a baby that had not touched the earth plain, a connection with mining; all ambiguous, none specific. The Psychic dustbin swallowed the lot. The medium's next link was much better, causing quite a reaction from the recipient.

"I've got a man here; calls himself *Digger*. Proper name Trevor says he's got a message for Elsie. Can anyone take this gentleman?"

He looked around the room for any response.

"I can. *But I won't*," said Mrs. Elsie Flint, a stalwart of the committee who was in charge of the tea and biscuits. "And he *certainly* wasn't a gentleman."

The congregation's attention was restored, the fidgeting stopped, what next?

"He says he's very sorry for all the arguments and the way he treated you. He asks for your forgiveness."

"He can ask all day long, but he *won't* get it. Horrible man. Selfish to the core."

Elsie's outburst totally surprised the medium, who was desperate to extricate himself from the complicated and unpleasant marital problems Digger and Elsie had shared. He needed to break the embarrassing ethereal connection; sooner than later.

"He says you have a picture of him on the sideboard."

"I keep it there to remind me of the bad times. If I feel down and sorry for myself, I just look at his self righteous image and think myself lucky to be rid of him. It works wonders; picks me up no end. He never made me feel that good when he was alive."

Miriam suppressed her amusement at the exposé of the Flint family domestic problems by holding a handkerchief tightly to her mouth. She turned to her daughter to see what effect this unusual Spiritual revelation was having on her.

Julia couldn't believe the little old tea lady. She looked like butter wouldn't melt in her mouth, but by golly she was feisty. "He must have led her a right merry dance," she said to her mum, fighting back the giggles.

The congregation, with one exception, Mrs. Barrows, whose hearing aid had decided to act up, loudly responded to the entertainment provided by Mrs. Flint and Mr. Flint, deceased. Laughter exploded to a new level when the embarrassed Minister Jim Higgins slowly turned to Annie, saying, "He's gone now; shall we close?"

"*Well Elsie*, you certainly made that a service to remember," Annie congratulated the star of the show, now busy carrying out her kitchen duties.

"I don't care," she said lining up the rows of tea cups ready for the thirsty customers, "I had to *live* with him. People don't know the half of it. He treated me like a skivvy. I had no choice when he was down here. But he can sod off now."

"Two please, one without milk," Julia interrupted. "And good for you, passing over don't automatically turn you into a Saint."

"The Lord may have absolved him for all that he's done, *but I don't*. It's his turn to suffer now. *And there's an end to it*. Sugar pot is over there if you want any."

Annie joined the refreshments queue. "Are you looking forward to Tuesday Miriam?"

"I am; but the prayer bit is bothering me."

Annie put her hand on Miriam's shoulder, "You'll be fine. Dolly will look after you. She won't expect miracles you know. She was a beginner herself not too long ago."

"I know. But anyway, I'll do my best." Miriam sipped her tea.

"No one can ask for more my dear, is Fred coming?"

"I think so. I know he's interested. I caught him reading the library book Julia got me. He put it down quickly when I walked in, but I know Fred, he's a dark horse, much deeper than you think."

"Good. We need a man in the circle. Helps to balance out the energies. Women only groups are really bad news. Too much influence on make-up and fashion. It brings out the bitch in all of us."

I know just what you mean, Miriam nodded; gazing in wonderment at Annie's magnificent posterior.

"That made a change Julia. I don't know about you, but in my opinion Mrs. Flint's contact with Spirit was as plausible as any other I've witnessed. No relationship can be a bunch of roses all of the time. We accept our friends and loved ones, warts and all, on this side of life, why should things change when they pass over?"

"*Precisely!*" Julia was warming to the conversation. "If a Medium told me Grandma Haslam came through with anything nice to say about me I'd be very sceptical. I know we all want nice positive uplifting messages from the Spirit World, but I'd sooner have honest down to earth proof than the goody goody flannel and soft soap rubbish some of them give you. Some of the stuff is obviously fabricated to please the recipient."

Mother and daughter said goodnight to a few of the church members and made their way to the car.

Annie was in the driveway helping Mrs. Barrows into a taxi. "See you both on Tuesday, don't be late."

Mrs. Barrows turned to Annie and said, "You don't have to shout, I'm not *deaf.*"

Chapter 13

"Well Frankie, you'll never believe it, I've joined the Spookies." Fred was talking to one of his racing pigeons, named after Frankie Dettori; the best jockey in the world.

Early, dawn breaking, Fred just had to tell somebody; couldn't discuss it with Harry, his Ladbrokes partner and workmate of long standing, not yet anyway, early days, could ruin a good friendship.

"Yeah, I can't believe it meself. Who'd have thought it? I'm not a full member mind ya, provisional sorta. I need a lot more evidence before *I* accept what they say about dying. Us Sagittarians aren't easily converted. *Proof*, that'll do it, nowt else. It's a good job I'm retired, the lads at A Winning Colliery wouldn't half have gin' me some stick."

Frankie cooed, picked up some seed and stared at Fred.

****

Last year's mysterious avian epidemic had decimated the local pigeon fancy, robbing Fred of most of his young birds. Only the weekend before Jeremy's fatal accident father and son had thoroughly cleaned out and disinfected the loft, talked about entering the surviving young birds in the RPRA One Loft Races.

Frankie was the only adult cock left in the loft. Always Fred's favourite bird; his pet. Never quite good enough to win any races, but a trier, always a trier. He'd fly till he dropped. Four years old, now relegated to being a show bird.

Fred lost all interest in the hobby since Jeremy died, eventually advertising the loft for sale in the Pigeon Racing Weekly.

Frankie, Fred had decided, was staying, his new residence a parrot cage, to stand on the work bench in the garden shed.

Miriam hung out the washing, interrupting her husband's tete-a-tete with his feathered friend.

"Is it time for a tea break love?"

"Yes Fred. Shall I bring it outside?"

The garden was a haven for wildlife. Squirrels ran across the lawn, displaying acrobatic skills worthy of any gymnast. Robins hopped about, chasing the wrens and sparrows away from the scattered bread crumbs. Great tits hung from the seed feeders, hastily zooming off as Fred and Miriam sat down for their elevenses.

"I love this garden," Miriam said. "It's like time stands still. It's so peaceful. I could stay here forever."

Fred wasn't listening, too busy thinking . "Walter's picking up the young pigeons on Friday. He'll give 'em a good home."

"Well I for one won't miss 'em," Miriam sniffled. "I'm sorry Fred, but they were always pooing on my washing."

"Any road, don't matter now, they're going." He was close to tears.

"Fred?"

"What?"

"Next Thursday is the Anniversary."

"I know."

"Jeremy's passing."

"I know."

"I don't believe it. You forget birthdays but you've remembered our Jeremy's passing."

"*Yeah* . That's far more important. He was me only *son*, and he's gone."

"He was *our* son. There's not a day goes by I don't think of him. I'm the one on the tablets. I don't hear you crying yourself to sleep every night."

"I wish I could, then perhaps this pain would go from me guts. I can't sleep without dreaming about the accident. I wake up in a cold sweat, heart pumping. That's why I sleep in the spare room."

"I thought it was because I snored. *You said so*."

"Just an excuse. You *do* snore. But so what. I could've slept on my good ear and I wouldn't have heard a thing."

"*Oh Fred*. I wished you'd told me."

"I can only tell ya now because of the Spiritualist stuff. I've noticed a big change in you and our Julia. Even though I've only been to the one circle meeting, I'm already looking at our loss differently. Mind ya, *the book helped*."

"I don't believe it. You sneaky sod."

"If you keep saying 'I don't believe it' they'll be callin' you Victor. Stop it will ya."

"Seriously Fred, I'm really glad you told me what you did just now." Miriam grabbed and squeezed his hand. Not one for exhibiting emotion, especially with Fred, the Sagittarian, she felt good about it. And by his look so did Fred.

"Y'know Fred, together we can get through this turmoil. I don't expect to completely stop crying when I think of our lad, but I'm certain it will get easier; for both of us. Sorry. I should say the three of us. Our Julia's still as devastated as we are."

"Poor gel. She's had it rough. First the baby then her brother. Really distressing. She wanted a son. I know she did."

"You *knew*."

"Of course I did. *Do ya think I'm that stupid?* She wasn't very big, I'll give ya that, but even I knew she was pregnant. Ya don't throw up like she did unless you're with child or dying from gastroelephantosis. "

"I made that word up. There's no medical description for the

68

projectile vomiting she produced. Olympic standard I'd say."

"Julia didn't want you to know. I had to promise not to say anything." Miriam cocked back in her seat, giving him a long, hard look. "I've learnt a lot about you today Mr. Frederick William Brooks. I don't know if you're deep or devious, or whatever. Tell you what, I'll give you the benefit of the doubt and stick with deep."

"Do us a favour, love. Will ya tell Julia I know. It'll come better from you."

"It's no good avoiding these emotional issues. Once faced they're not too bad."

"*You stand need to talk*. Ya can't even say DEAD."

"I'm getting there. Slowly perhaps. But surely. You must've seen some improvement."

"Yeah. True." Fred put his favourite mug down, it held a full pint. 'A mug for a Mug,' his friend Harry had said when presenting it to Fred for his sixtieth birthday. "Nice drop o' tea that. Ta. As for getting better I'd say ya are. Thank goodness. *Ya had me so worried*. When Doctor Mazzimo prescribed them sedatives it frightened me. My mate Knocker Young's mum had them when she suffered with her anxiety problems. She was on another planet whenever I saw her. Horrible to see her like that. Such a lovely woman. The sooner ya get off them things the better."

"I will. I know I will. I've got all the help I need now. Julia, you and our Jeremy, I know he's around me. Somewhere close. I know that Fred. I just do."

"Let's take it a bit at a time gel. The circle is helping. Let's see what happens at tomorra's gathering. On Thursday we'll all go to Crem, assuming Julia wants ta come."

"She'll come. I'm not sure if Harry will be able to make it. He's doing a big project for Unichem at the moment. There's another cup of tea in the pot; pass your mug." Miriam poured the last of the tea and paused to listen. "*Hey, don't robins sing lovely?* Nature's so wonderful. We really don't appreciate it as we should do we?"

"Ta love." Fred took the offered mug. "No, we sure don't."

Chapter 14

"Well, it's nice to see you all again. Have you remembered the pen and paper?"

Dolly, as thin as ever, waited patiently as the ladies scuffled inside their handbags. Fred pulled a notebook from his jacket pocket, inducing quite a titter when a handful of betting slips scattered across the floor.

"Thank you Fred, but I'm not taking bets yet on who'll get the first Spirit message."

Dolly's remark set them giggling; the atmosphere in the little church instantly lifted. Such a sense of humour infused the building and its occupants with positive, friendly energy. An excellent omen for the rest of the night.

"I've decided to rearrange the seating plan. I may have to do this a few times before I'm happy." Dolly gestured here and there, outlining her ideas. "It's all about the flow of energy around the circle. I'll know when it's right. *Annie* can you swop with Doris please?"

"I've got some extra pens if anybody needs one; courtesy of Ladbrokes." Fred put his cap on the floor, pulled a few of the trademark red pens out of his pocket and offered them out.

"Thanks Fred. Can I have one please, my Biro's packed up."

Summer took the pen and sat in her designated chair.

At seven fifteen the circle opened. Pencils, pens and papers lay at the feet of their owners.

"*Miriam* will open in prayer. Please send her your love and support. Just say it from the heart Miriam," Dolly was firm, "we *don't* expect the sermon from the mount, not yet."

Miriam stood, hesitated a little, it being her first go, cleared her throat then started, "Our Father God, please bless us all. Watch over us and protect us. Allow us to find the knowledge we all seek.

Amen."

Miriam sat again, still shaking from her first attempt at Public Speaking; the experience quite daunting. She couldn't imagine how it felt to address a large audience. Having intended to say more, much more, the words dried up. Next time she'd be better. Fingers crossed.

"Thank you Miriam. That was fine." Praise where it's due, Dolly felt. *"Tonight's* meditation will be different. I'm taking you on a Spiritual excursion. I want you to mentally visualise the journey in every detail. See the images, hear the sounds, smell the fragrances; notice all that surrounds and enfolds you. When I bring you back, write down all you've experienced. Do it as quickly as possible. It's surprising how fast you forget things."

Even before Dolly started the meditation five of the students were eagerly waiting, all relaxed, ready and willing to welcome the experience.

Doris was the exception. She wondered why she'd been moved. Sitting next to Summer somehow felt *awkward*. It wasn't the age difference. Indeed old enough to be the girl's grandmother; it *wasn't* that.

"Close your eyes. Feel the calmness envelop you. See the white shield of protection fortifying our group. You're grounded, safe, and open to Spirit. As you go deeper into the silence you'll be aware of the changes. You're no longer in this room. You're walking along a path. It's narrow and cuts through a glorious expanse of daffodils. They stand tall and proud, as if guarding you on your way. Tufts of short green grass soften your tread. You feel the warmth of the sun, shining through the clearest blue sky. A swallow weaves through the air; dipping its wings into the golden carpet of daffodils. All is well.

"In the distance you see a small building. As you get nearer you see that it's a cottage, surrounded by a pure white picket fence; a gate in the middle stands wide open, inviting you to enter. A robin sits to one side, watching you; deep red chest puffed out, proudly welcoming you to this haven of tranquility. The feathered sentry permits you to place your hand within inches of its small delicate body.

"The smell of lavender hits you as you enter the front garden. Three steps and you face the wooden door. It isn't locked. Turning the smooth round handle you enter.

"The room is small. A single window on your left is enough to illuminate the whole interior. A large open fireplace takes up most of the wall facing you. Wood burns in the grate, flames wave to you as they vanish up the chimney."

Dolly quickly looked around the circle, hopeful the enchantment worked.

Yes, I've got all of them.

"You find the armchair to your right and sink into it's welcoming softness. You are totally at peace. Content. The warmth of the fire caresses your body. You could stay forever, comfortable and safe. This is your sanctuary. Your refuge. All is well. You have total control. Nothing can harm you in this magical realm. Here you can blend with Spirit; communicate on your terms. Only the good, friendly, loving energies, are allowed entry. I'll leave you now to enjoy the serenity."

They all looked dead. Even Doris was away with the fairies. Fred's head slumped on his chest, mouth wide open like a fish, arms dangling at his side, almost touching the crumpled cap lying at his feet. Bless him.

The other four looked like Angels, the stillness of their faces broken only by gentle smiles, appearing and fading away in cycles.

Ten minutes passed. Dolly decided another few minutes and she'd bring them back.

Then all plans disintegrated. Dolly's attention was drawn to Summer. Subtle, but definite changes distorted her features. Her mouth seemed wider, thinner; her nose was certainly altered, the nostrils flared, looked more masculine.

Alarm bells rang in Dolly's head.

Oh my God, the realisation frightened her; *she's being overshadowed*. I must do something, quickly.

"It's now time to make your way home," Dolly said hurriedly. "Say your farewells to anyone present and leave the cottage. Bring with you any information or advice you've received and find the path home."

Yes, much faster than she'd planned. The shortcut was unfortunate but so necessary.

"Feel the vibration change. Become more aware of the energies. You can sense your physical body. You notice your breathing. Slow and relaxed. You feel the firmness of the chair. You are now *awake*. Fully aware of the now. Back with your friends."

Oh dear, not good to bring them back like that; they could get the Spirit equivalent of the bends. Nastier than the diver's version, with no remedial decompression chamber at hand.

Too fast. Much too fast.

"*Are you alright Summer?*" Dolly asked, one hand either side of the girl's face.

Summer's eyes looked glazed. "I feel a bit shaky. What happened?"

"I've only seen it on one occasion," Dolly explained. "*You were overshadowed*. A few more minutes and you'd have provided the first full blown demonstration of physical transfiguration I'd witnessed outside of Stansted. It so nearly happened."

"*Is that bad?*"

"It's wonderful. *But not in these circumstances.* Precautions *have* to be implemented. Strict control has to be maintained. It can be so dangerous. You could've been hurt. Seriously hurt."

"Helen Duncan never recovered you know. I read all about it in that library book." Julia shared her knowledge of the disastrous séance with her puzzled friends.

"*Wow,*" Summer exclaimed. "I knew it was different. More real than last week. It was like watching a TV programme in my head."

"That's your third eye love," Dolly explained.

"That's funny, Miriam's is in the back of her head," Fred said with a wink to his partner.

"One more quip like that and the chip pan is *definitely* a gonner." Miriam was not amused.

Julia gave her dad a dirty look, then turned her attention to what Summer was saying.

"I loved it in that cottage." Summer looked radiant in the telling. "It's magic. After you left us there I had a lovely time. Grandpa Jack came in. He was such a nice man. Always a tube of Smarties at Grandpa's. He looked just the same as last time I saw him. Must be nearly ten years since he died; he'd not altered a bit. Just the same. Still wore his old trilby."

"Did Grandpa say anything?" Dolly questioned the excited girl.

"He said he loved me; that he was always there for me."

"You see, that's true love, unconditional love." Dolly was touched, close to tears by Summer's experience. "They say it moves mountains; it does more than that, it brings the two worlds together. *Ours and theirs.*"

Dolly sat down. "He's your guardian and doorkeeper Summer. He'll help you no end. But be careful, he's so powerful, he can completely overshadow you, and that's dangerous. Unless you're working with experienced people that you trust. Tell him to back off. He *must* respect your safety. That comes first; always."

Summer felt a tiny chill. She nodded in what she hoped was a positive gesture to let Dolly know she'd understood the veiled warning.

*****

The visualisation experiment was a great success. Fred thought the cottage was a great place. He'd sat in the chair simply enjoying the peace and quiet. The open fire reminded him of his childhood. Good times. When called back to consciousness he'd returned reluctantly, yet could easily have stayed.

Annie had a similar experience and was very satisfied.

"Uplifted and recharged," she commented.

"Did you get anything Doris?" Dolly asked, fearing the worst.

"Not as much as last week," she replied tersely. "I just sat in the chair, it was very uncomfortable. I was glad to come back."

Dolly didn't give Doris a chance to say more. "Miriam, how about you?"

"I loved every minute. The flowers, the robin, the lavender, that's my favourite fragrance. I use it everywhere don't I Julia?"

"Yes Mum. *Everywhere.*"

"The fire was gorgeous." Miriam's face glowed. "After a while I got out of the chair and sat on the floor; I was looking into the flames when you brought us back."

"Good. I am pleased for you." Dolly turned, "That leaves you Julia."

"Same as Mum really. Except for one thing. I'm sure someone was with me. I didn't see or hear anything, but I did smell something. *Old Spice.*"

"You *didn't* our Julia. Are you sure?" Miriam's smile

wavered.

"Yes *Mum*, I'm *sure*, Old Spice."

"Am I missing something here *ladies?*" Dolly looked from one to the other.

Fred answered first, "Our Jeremy always wore it. He's our son, or was. He never went out without a splash of Old Spice. We teased him rotten about it. A young lad like him using that vintage stuff. Are ya sure it were Old Spice? Lynx smells very similar."

"*DAD.*"

Dolly clapped her hands. "Julia that's wonderful. I'm so pleased for you and the family. I'd heard about your tragedy from Annie. I'm sure with more practice and patience you could make a stronger connection."

"Now, Miriam, can you close please. We've done enough for tonight."

This time, because of the way she felt, Miriam stood taller somehow. Confident and assured that she would find the words, the right ones to close the meeting. "Thank you Lord for watching over us. We've shared a brief time with the Spirit World and are uplifted by the evidence, the proof, that life and love are eternal. I ask for a blessing on each of us and the homes that we represent. Watch over and protect us until we meet again. Amen."

"Thank you Miriam. *Much* better." Dolly rested a hand on Doris's shoulder. "Next week It's your turn my dear. Until then, have a safe journey home. Oh and do bring the pen and paper again, in tonight's excitement none of you used them."

"Dolly?"

"Yes Julia."

"Do you think I could make the link at home, would Jeremy come through if Mum and Dad helped me?"

"You never know what might happen in meditation. It's always an experiment, same as medium-ship. If Spirit doesn't want to work with you, tough, end of demonstration."

"But I almost made the contact, didn't I? *Smelling the aftershave.*"

"Yes you did, and I'm so pleased for you. I'm sure in time you will make the link. But look at it this way, tonight you were part of a circle of immense inner strength, most of the power generated by Annie, Summer and myself. This battery pack of energy helped you make that brief contact. Compare this to what your family, indeed all novices at this moment in time, can produce. I know your intentions are good, the heart is in it Julia, but realistically I would have to say no. It seems to be an impossible task. Sorry." Dolly saw exuberance drain from Julia's face.

"Thanks for being honest. We just want it so much. My brother was snatched from us, before any of us could say goodbye."

"Time is a great healer, love. The pain will lessen. Take heart from tonight. He's around you. We've had the proof. But just out of reach… *for now.*"

Chapter 15

Miriam placed the Arum lilies in the vase, carefully arranging them as best she could, then joined Julia and Fred in the Quiet Room at the Crematorium.

"I wish I could write like that, it's beautiful." Miriam admired the entry in the Book of Remembrance.

"Worth every penny," Julia sa id. "It looks like it was written in the middle ages. The *colours* are fabulous. What do you think Dad?"

Fred stood next to the locked display cabinet, leaning gently against the frame.

"It's really nice that is. Fit for a king. No one could ask for more. God bless him."

"Read it to us Dad, please."

Fred shifted position. He cleared his throat.

"'Jeremy Albert Brooks, loving son and faithful brother. A bright light in a dark world. 1971 - 2006. Always missed. Never forgotten. '"

Fred wrapped his big arms around wife and daughter; it felt funny, but good.

They all cried, together.

"Dad."

"Yeah love."

"I'm sorry."

"*Wott for* lass."

"Losing the baby."

"Silly gel. Don't let me ever hear you say that again. It wasn't your fault. It happens. Yer weren't the first, yer won't be the last. Don't go blaming yourself. Hear me, just don't, okay?"

"I should've told you before now Dad. Sorry."

Miriam stepped between them.

"Let that be an end to it. Both of you; silly buggers. And you Fred Brooks, here, wipe your eyes. The last time I saw you cry was when you buried them dead pigeons. Come on, let's walk round the gardens. It's lovely here."

Mansfield crematorium was busy. It always was.

The Brooks family came out of the Remembrance Room as yet another funeral party arrived. Both chapels would be in action; eight services were listed today.

"Look at the squirrel over there next to the path?" Julia pointed to the fluffy tailed entertainer scurrying across the grass, totally oblivious to its surroundings, or the emotional procedures carried out in the vicinity.

"Aw, ain't that sad." Fred had halted to inspect the flowers left for one recent departee. "Look Miriam, only two wreaths, one from the Nursing Home, other from the Miners' Welfare. Poor gel, I guess she had no relatives. I bet she played Bingo at Welfare."

"Different to that one." Julia pointed. "Must be at least twenty arrangements over there; don't seem right somehow."

They walked through the well-kept grounds, absorbing the peace and quiet. Even the trees seemed to respect the location. Bouquets and wreaths were wrapped around several trunks; other sections of ground had bare patches where the ashes of loved ones had been sprinkled.

The trio stopped by a solitary willow. Bowing their heads they formed a circle, nothing was said. Miriam grasped the silver chain round her neck, fighting back the tears.

"A lot's happened since last year," Fred broke the silence. "Next year will be even better. Cum, let's move on."

"Have you noticed these plaques Fred? They go all around the pond; I wonder if we should have one for our Jeremy."

"I looked at 'em, I'm not impressed. If you look around the

back edge there's quite a few hanging off. Only been there a few years, check the dates on 'em."

 "Oh yeah, this one's only been on for four years," Miriam observed.

"The commemorative bushes look nice Mum, look at that one, Mr. Squirrel seems to like it."

"Fred, when we go, call in the office and pick up a brochure."

"I'll do that love."

They finished the tour of the grounds.

A procession of black limousines crept silently down the drive, appearing reluctant to part with their cargo.

"Another one coming in," Fred corrected himself, "should say going out really."

"They've been gone awhile, Dad. This part of the process is only for us that are left behind; our way of saying goodbye. We come here to pay our respects."

"True. I'm beginning to see things clearer now meself; Jeremy ain't here at all. We scattered his ashes beside that weeping willow in the corner but he aint there. Not actually there."

"What a difference from last year. I was saying to Mum that I was dreading today. You were as well, weren't you Mum?"

"I had to take a tablet before we set out, I knew it would be a challenge. But after your dad read the inscription, and we shed a few tears, I felt much better. Like a big weight had been lifted from my heart. That's Spiritualism for you, I know it."

"Dad."

"Yeah." Fred started the car, put it in gear and eased down the drive towards the gates.

"Why don't you come to church on Sunday, give us your honest opinion. Annie and Doris will be there, you'll love the tea lady, won't he Mum?"

"He won't come," Miriam chimed in from the back seat. She

wouldn't sit next to Fred, all too aware he constantly chuntered on about women drivers. She'd have slapped him before long; best let Julia enjoy the pleasure of his company.

"Will you Dad? *Go on*, come with us, please."

"I'll miss me tea."

"*I told you*. Him and his belly!"

Fred jumped on the brakes, Julia jerked forward, held in place by the seat belt.

"*Silly bugger*," Miriam squealed from the back. "I've just eaten my breakfast again. Be more careful."

Fred didn't like the criticism. "I nearly hit that bloody dog. Give it a rest both on ya. I can't concentrate when you two are gettin' on at me."

"I *told* you he wouldn't, Julia."

A deep sigh rattled out of Fred. "*Anything for a quiet life.* I'll bloody go. Are ya satisfied now?"

"It's a miracle, a miracle."

"You sound like a bloody Evangelist's TV advert," Fred shouted into the rear view mirror.

"You sound like another one, Men behaving badly." Miriam would have the last word.

"If ya don't shut up Julia will be driving, I nearly went through a red light then."

"Do you mean it Dad? You will go."

"On one condition."

"Be careful Fred. Your *daughter's* present," Miriam chimed.

"Silly woman, behave. The condition is simply this, tell me where ya've hid the chip pan; I've looked everywhere."

Miriam almost choked with laughter, "I knew you'd never find it. I put it in the shed, next to the lawn mower, I've been asking you for weeks to mow the back lawn. I ended up doing the sodding thing again, as usual. Men; who'd have 'em?"

Chapter 16

"What a pleasant surprise, all the family; how nice."

"It wasn't easy so don't ask." Miriam bought three strips of raffle tickets from Annie then led the way to the back row of Hasland Church; left side. It was starting to become a habit.

"Shall I sit between ya."

"Very chivalrous I'm *sure*, Mr. Brooks. You must be after something but thank you anyway," Miriam winked.

"*Sarci again*," Fred huffed.

Miriam scowled.

"Ya can't accept it as a nice gesture can ya. Silly woman?"

"*Stop it you two*," Julia demanded. "*Remember where you are.*" To be honest she was tired of their bickering.

"I stick out like a sore thumb. I'm the only bloke here."

"You might be less conspicuous if you take that cap off," Miriam hissed.

"Hang on a bit Dad, there's five minutes to go yet; Mr. Manston always cuts it fine. He'll be here, won't he Mam?"

"I bet he will. He goes round with the collection plate; some relation of Doris Clarke's; on her mum's side."

Mrs. Clarke, although she was the President, reluctantly chaired. Annie having done it for the last four weeks.

"Enough," she said, "let somebody else have a go. You rarely get a message if you chair. It looks bad if you do. People start saying it's fixed." Prior knowledge gained apparently from sitting together in the medium's room.

Mrs. Clarke's somewhat shrill tone cut through the indistinct muttering of the congregation. "Please make sure that your mobiles are switched off. We only want messages from the Spirit World thank you." A wide smile hovered before she continued, "I would like to introduce Celia Farlowe from Doncaster; I'm sure that we'll have a lovely service. Please give her a warm welcome."

A smattering of applause crawled through.

"I've had warmer welcomes in the Conservative Club."

"Shush Fred, behave yourself."

"She's a comely lass right enough. Does she do private sittings?"

"*I'm not bringing you again.* You can stay at home with the soddin' Spam sandwiches."

The first hymn was the popular evergreen, *How great thou art.*

"That's a good tune, I liked that. Seems ta, I dunno quite how ta put it, lift ya to a higher level, inside." Fred felt more at ease by the minute.

Miss Farlowe wasn't a day over thirty. Small, slim, and almost pretty, attired very elegantly in a modest turquoise dress. Her prayer was adequate, though hardly helped by a soft voice that failed to carry beyond the front row. Mrs. Barrows frantically shook her hearing aid, two old ladies on the end of the back row to the right looked at each other, mouthing, 'What did she say.'

The address was dismal but thankfully short. The second hymn was an absolute gem.

Doris had chosen a beauty. No one knew the tune and no one knew the words, not even Doris. The congregation of thirty sounded like twenty nine had gone home and the remaining one mumbled, quietly.

"Is it always this exciting Miriam?"

"*You're* being sarci now Fred. Shut up and give her a chance. It's not easy up there."

"How do ya know? You've never been on the platform."

"Saying them prayers in the circle opened my eyes. Wait till it's your turn." Miriam looked smug; she couldn't wait to see her nearest and dearest perform.

"I might be sick that week." For sure he'd find some excuse.

"*Coward*."

"I'll hand the rest of the service over to Celia," Miss Clarke announced. "Please send her your love and support."

The guest medium stepped up, visually swept the whole room then started. "I don't know exactly where I'm going, can anyone take a Humphrey."

"What, down here, in the physical?" A lady on the front row inquired.

"No madam, all my messages are from the dead."

"I can. But he wasn't related to me." Annie was pleased to be involved, at last.

"*I didn't say he was*. He's telling me he was a neighbour of yours, many years ago. Next door but one he's saying."

"Oh yes, Mr. Brown. Yes, a lovely man. I was only a young girl. He died when I was still in school. He kept pigeons."

"I was just about to tell you that." Miss Farlowe stiffened a little, pushed her glasses higher up her nose then continued.

"Sorry." Annie slithered down her seat. She should have known better.

"I'm feeling quite breathless with this gentleman. Did he suffer with his chest?"

"I'm not sure; I was only thirteen when he died. But he worked down the pit."

"That explains his conditions. He's making my chest feel tight, difficult to breathe. Take it away please Spirit. Thank you."

Recovering from her obvious discomfort the medium continued.

"He's come to say thank you."

"What for?" Annie looked surprised. "I didn't do anything."

"He says you helped him with his shopping. You'd run to the

corner shop for his bread and things."

"Oh, I'd forgotten that."

"*He hasn't*. Take his love with you and throw the stick away."

"*What?*"

"I don't know what he means. I'm just repeating his words. He says he has a bloke with him, and *he* wants you to throw the stick away."

Annie's face lit up. "Thank you so much Celia. Tell him I will, and bless him."

"Thank *you* for working with me love, I'm leaving you now."

"How about that Fred, she's a better medium than philosopher."

"Impressive. I'll give her that much."

"I feel that I'm over there, the lady in blue." Delia turned slightly. "There's a light over you my darling."

"*Me*. Are you sure?" The timid Mrs. Andrews turned her head, looking for the light.

"Work with me please and we'll see if I'm right. Have you a child in Spirit?"

A nod.

"A girl child, no more than a year old?"

Another nod.

"Darling you must *speak* to me. It's like following a car with one of those Churchill dogs in the back. Nods don't work here my love; we need your voice. *Spirit need the verbal link*, the energy. It's hard enough for them as it is." The glasses had another nudge.

"Yes. She was only ten months old," Mrs. Andrews said. "Diphtheria, a lot died that year; 1947."

"She's alright now. No problems at all. A lovely little woman is looking after her. She's the image of you. Just a bit different round the nose."

"That's Mum." Mrs. Andrews smiled and gave another nod.

"Thank you so much."

"Don't thank me my love, I'm only the go-between. *Thank Spirit.*"

"I will, and Bless you."

"Time for one more message Celia." Doris kept a tight ship, her philosophy being time is time, and she had a bus to catch.

"*Right.*" Celia said, "I know I'm on the back row. The gentleman with the check shirt." She looked his way. "*Yes, you Sir*, don't be shy; please work with me will you?"

"*Me. Are ya sure?*" Fred answered, gazing about him to check if there might be another likely candidate. And perhaps praying Celia had made a mistake.

"Yes. Give me your voice and we'll do just fine. I've got another link with pigeons. I hope you can take it. I don't want them."

"I know what you mean Celia, dirty little things," Miriam jumped in with her two pennyworth, "they ruin your washing."

"Just so. Are you three together?"

"I wouldn't sit next to him if we weren't."

"*Mum.* Behave."

Good natured laughter echoed through the building; you could feel the positive vibrations. Good old Miriam.

"No domestics please; save it till you get home. Now then, these pigeons; they look dead to me. Am I right?"

"*Could be,*" Fred reluctantly admitted. "*Are they Fantails?*"

"*Fred.* Behave." Miriam tapped his hand as one would a naughty schoolboy. "You know she's right. Don't be so stubborn."

"*Awright.* I did have a few die, yeah." He scowled.

"A young man is telling me there were six of them, that it was an epidemic of some sort. You had to disinfect everything; is that correct?"

"A lot of people knew that. Federation sent some men down to inspect our loft."

"I'll go back and ask for more. He's talking about a Frankie. He was all right. Frankie was all right, he says yes."

Julia's jaw dropped. So did Miriam's. Recovering herself Julia said, "Is that good enough for you then Dad? Or would you like more proof? Like the registration number on Frankie's ring, or how many races he had."

"That's my bird alright," Fred admitted, gob-smacked. "*How do ya know that?"*

"This young man is telling me sir. Is it correct?"

"Yes it is." Miriam interrupted. "Oh bless you Celia. You've got my Jeremy, my son. God bless you."

Celia shook her head. "He hasn't told me his name yet. Sometimes they don't."

"*Is he okay?"* Fred asked, unable to contain himself since the truth of the message had smacked him in the face. Miriam and Julia grabbed an arm each to keep him in his seat.

"Fine. He's fine. He had to stay on the first level when he got there. The Spirit World's equivalent to a convalescent home. Sort of."

"*Is he happy?"* Miriam stood up, handkerchief at the ready.

Celia, a mother herself, felt a real affinity with this woman. "Once you're up there all earthly values end. We all return to pure energy, the essence remains; the wrapping disappears."

The tears ran freely down Miriam's face. "Tell him I love him, please tell him. I always will. I'll never forget him."

"He knows that, remember this; love never dies. He'll always be a part of you, and you a part of him."

Julia cuddled up to her Dad, grasped his hand.

"I'm keeping Frankie, in me shed. In a cage. A big cage. *Tell him that will ya."*

Celia smiled, she loved these connections. The man receiving the communication was not the usual church attendee. She spotted them a mile away. Arms crossed, *'prove it to me'* written all over their faces.

"*He knows*. He's always around. He says he was with you the other day. 'You read it nice Dad', he's saying; 'you read it very nice.' I assume you know what that means? I don't. He's pleased that you're supporting each other. *The ties that bind*. Always."

Fred pulled his hankie out, blew a loud blast on his nose then sobbed on Julia's shoulder.

Miriam sat down, joined her husband and daughter in irrepressible crying.

It *would* get better now, for all of them.

"The link's fading, I can only just hear him. 'See you on Tuesday,' he keeps saying 'see you on Tuesday.' He's gone."

It was over. The link severed.

Celia watched the Brooks family, huddled together, sharing their moment of disclosure. Happiness and sadness entwined in equal measures.

Doris stood, "I'd like to thank Miss Celia Farlowe for coming all the way from Doncaster. I'm sure you'll all agree we've had a wonderful service. Whilst we're singing the closing hymn *God of the granite, Mr. Manston*, will you go round with the collection please? All free-will offerings are much appreciated thank you."

The closing prayer was a repeat of the opening one. Bland and forgetful.

"You forgot to give the notices Doris." Annie reminded.

Doris retaliated with, "You hadn't put the sheet on the lectern."

"Never mind, good service; Miss Farlowe can come again."

Composure recovered, Miriam and her family joined the queue

for refreshments.

They took the tea and biscuits back to their seats, sitting together in silence.

"*You* had a good message Fred." Annie placed a hand on his shoulder.

"Yeah. The best. Sure answered a lot of questions. Didn't it gels?"

"I feel so relieved, don't you Julia?" Miriam's hand trembled, her cup rattled.

"More than that Mum; I feel so positive. Any proof of life eternal is wonderful, but from our Jeremy, it's so special; invigorating. I'm so full up with it all."

"*Can we go now*?" It was a plea from Fred. "I'm hungry; me belly thinks me throat's cut."

Wife and daughter guessed what was coming before he said it.

"Trust you Mr. Brooks," Miriam laughed, she couldn't be angry in the aftermath of the wonderful validation Celia had produced. "Let's get you home before you completely wither away."

Julia walked slowly behind her parents, smiling at everyone.

The Brooks family left Hasland Spiritualist Church in high spirits, literally; Fred and Miriam holding hands until they reached the car, as if something had been rekindled.

****

"Tell you what," Miriam said, switching the kettle on, "Celia's *mediumship* was fantastic. But her prayers and philosophy were rather poor."

"*Mum*, are you *criticising her,* after the *message* we had? Come on, be fair."

Miriam realised she may have exaggerated her misgivings.

"Not really criticising, just commenting Julia. Twenty odd people didn't get a message tonight. Only second hand proof ; reflected from us lucky ones."

"*So?*"

"Well, if the philosophy had been good, and interesting of course, everyone would have got something, a piece of advice, a word of encouragement maybe. We all need help in one way or another. Coping with the loss of a loved one is so tough, as well we know; just a thought I had. I'm probably being ungrateful, and out of order."

"The medium's the attraction Mum, the link with the Higher Realms. We all want a message from our loved ones."

"Ya both right y'know." Fred wanted his say. "A message from beyond the grave is the magnet. Yeah, of course it is. And God bless all mediums, like that lovely Celia Farlowe tonight, for bringing the evidence that death is not the end but a new beginning. *But consider this,* I never got a message in Dolly's circles, but I felt calmer and more content afterwards. As if I'd found somethin'. And I know for sure that's a lasting benefit. With a bit of practice I can use the meditation thing ta sort me out. I have many black days, thinking 'bout our Jeremy."

"*I'll sort you out* Freddy Brooks," Miriam laughed aloud. Julia joined in the infectious glee. Things were certainly getting better.

Miriam wiped away the tears of joy and continued, "I knew you had hidden depths Victor, and that's the last time I'll call you that. You're a changed man; there's a hidden philosopher inside that stubborn Sagittarian frame of yours." And she meant every word.

"Yeah, maybe so love. I do feel Spiritualism is a way of living, not just about getting messages from beyond the grave. Me outlook on life *is* changed, different from before."

"Does that mean the chip pan's going and Ladbrokes will be

losing a valuable customer?" Miriam went in for the kill.

He met her look with an equally challenging one. "Nah, don't be daft." He leaned closer and whispered, "tonight I'm moving back in ta front bedroom." He kissed her on the cheek.

Shocked but pleasantly surprised, Miriam nodded her acceptance, bound to state, "I'm warning you Fred, I might still wake up crying. It's still early days."

"Yeah, then we'll cry together love."

Epilogue

"Fred. Come quick. Frankie's being attacked." Miriam threw the
basket of clothes on the lawn, rushing to investigate the noisy
skirmish at the shed door.

Frankie had been careless, and unlucky. Spoiled by his keeper
he'd grown fat. Since the passing of the young man he often
roamed round the garden, free to fly, or not. The large cage in the
shed was always left open, more a sanctuary than a prison.

The Sparrowhawk knew no different. The plump pigeon looked
like a good meal, an easy target; not a pet to be overlooked and
spared.

The predator escaped at Miriam's first squeal. By the time Fred
reached the scene the winged instrument of death was two gardens
away, talons full of feathers and flesh, beak dripping with the life
blood of Frankie.

"Jeremy is waiting for ya Frankie," Fred cradled the bird in his
large hand like a baby. "He says ya can do owt ya want up there,
race against t' other pigeons or just rest int' loft, cooing to ya
hearts content. He'll come and see ya, just like old times."

"Is he alright Fred? Can I do anything?" Miriam guessed the
answer was no, on both counts.

"He wouldn't have suffered ya know. It woulda been over in a
few seconds." Fred decided to hide the mortal wounds inflicted on
his friend and confidant. It would serve no purpose, Miriam would
have been upset. No need for that. Not at all. Bad enough that he
should have to look at the gaping holes left in the throat and chest
of the beautiful Fantail he'd reared from a chick.

"Have ya got a shoe box darling? I want ta bury him over there,
in the lavender bed. I caught him strutting in the big clump in the
corner. He'd like t' rest there, I know he would."

"Oh Fred, I'm so sorry. I know how much you loved that bird.
You can have that Clarke's box I got on my last visit to
Meadowhall. Will that be OK?

Fred just nodded. It wasn't the time for talking. It was the time for crying; and he did.

****

"Fred."

"Yes love."

"Will you put this in the box with Frankie."

"What is it?"

Miriam took the silver chain and ring from around her neck, placing it like a Crown Jewel in his right hand.

"*Are ya sure*, it looks valuable ta me."

"It is. *Very valuable*. I bought it for our Jeremy's 36th birthday. He never got it of course. I want him to have it now."

"*Ya can't be serious darlin'. Ya ought ta keep it.*"

"No. Let it lie besides Frankie, bury them together, please. I'm serious. I know what I'm doing."

"Well I don't so tell us ya reasons gel."

"You'll think I'm being daft but I'm not bothered. It's symbolic."

"I *do* think tha being daft. *Symbolic*, what crap is that?" Fred put the box beside the hole, waiting for an answer.

"That there helped me through a crisis. It was my crutch, my armour, whichever. And yes, sometimes even confessional. I don't know how I'd have managed without it that first year."

"So *why* throw it in the grave with a dead pigeon? Ya never did like pigeons."

"Now *you're* being daft. Frankie wasn't just any pigeon, he was special. Jeremy was as fond of him as you were, you *know* that. I'm not doing this for me, it's for Jeremy."

"How can it be for our Jeremy?" Fred was shaking his head.

"I believe in life eternal, for the human race and the animal kingdom. Jeremy and Frankie are now reunited in Spirit. I know it. Symbolically I'm using Frankie to deliver the last present I bought our son, I don't need it anymore."

Fred didn't fully understand his wife's reasoning or motive, but a weird logic hung over the argument. He kissed the belated birthday present before placing it over Frankie's neck, securely

95

fastened the lid down with tie wraps then gently positioned the box in a framework of bricks. A concrete slab completed the miniature mausoleum. 'Frankie, may you fly with the Angels,' was written in marker pen.

"A fitting Epitaph." Fred hugged Miriam.

"Shall we have our tea outside Fred, make the most of the sunshine, we can have a ham salad if you like."

"Can ya make me a Spam salad please, and none of that low fat dressing stuff ya tried ta gimme last time."

"I'm having a sprinkling of Parmesan on my jacket potato, would you like some? It's organic."

"It smells organic, straight from the sewers. *Are ya tryin' ta kill me off?*"

"Not this week Fred, one funeral's enough thank you."

"You've got a warped sense of humour Miriam Mary; I'll warn our Julia about it the next time she comes ta visit."

"Oh, I forgot to tell you, she's coming over tonight."

"*Tonight*? It must be important, it's her Bingo night."

"If I tell you why she's coming you've got to promise me you'll look surprised when she tells you."

Fred stopped his feeding frenzy. "She's not getting divorced, is she now. Not from Harry; such a fine chap, reminds me so much of meself at his age."

"Don't be silly, your way out of line, although you've just mentioned sufficient grounds for a divorce, but that's not the issue."

Fred took off his cap, scratched his head and shot Miriam a gormless expression. "Ya could have done far worse ya know, Billy Murphy sure had the hots for ya."

"Stop it Fred, you're bringing up memories I'd sooner forget. I was only joking."

"So why's our gel coming tonight?"

"Promise you'll behave."

"I promise, tell us."

"She's pregnant." Miriam's face lit up like a super nova. She couldn't contain her joy at sharing the news.

Fred put his hat on, took Miriam's hands in his. "That's wonderful, couldn't have come at a better time. I've always fancied being a Grandad."

"She had the scan yesterday. Four months and everything's fine. She's got by the problem stage. Thank God. I shouldn't tell you anymore but I can't keep it to myself. She thinks it's a boy. Between you, me and that empty cage over there, if it is, she'll name it Frankie Jeremy Frederick."

"That's a right mouthful, don't ya think?"

"Sure is. Pass me your mug Grandad, let's celebrate."